A&E DRAMA

Blood pressure is high and pulses are racing
in these fast-paced dramatic stories from
Mills & Boon® Medical Romance™.
They'll move a mountain to save a life in an
emergency, be they the crash team, emergency
doctors, or paramedics. There are lots of
critical engagements amongst the high
tensions and emotional passions in these
exciting stories of lives and loves at risk!

When **Joanna Neil** discovered Mills & Boon®, her life-long addiction to reading crystallised into an exciting new career writing Medical Romance™. Her characters are probably the outcome of her varied lifestyle, which includes working as a clerk, typist, nurse and infant teacher. She enjoys dressmaking and cooking at her Leicestershire home. Her family includes a husband, son and daughter, an exuberant yellow Labrador and two slightly crazed cockatiels. She currently works with a team of tutors at her local education centre to provide creative writing workshops for people interested in exploring their own writing ambitions.

Recent titles by the same author:

HER BOSS AND PROTECTOR

BY
JOANNA NEIL

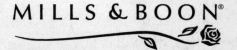

MILLS & BOON®

First published in Great Britain 2006
Harlequin Mills & Boon Limited,
Eton House, 18-24 Paradise Road, Richmond, Surrey TW9 1SR

© Joanna Neil 2006

ISBN 0 263 84725 X

Set in Times Roman 10½ on 12½ pt.
03-0406-50279

Printed and bound in Spain
by Litografia Rosés, S.A., Barcelona

CHAPTER ONE

'THIS is it, children. We're here.' Jade parked the car alongside the pavement and then went around to the passenger side to open the door and let the children out. 'Will you help me with some of the bags? Connor, perhaps you could bring in the toys and, Rebeccah, maybe you could manage the schoolbags?'

'Is this your house?' Four-year-old Connor stepped out of the car and looked the place over. He was frowning, his lip jutting a fraction, as though he was trying to decide what to make of it.

'Yes, it is, for the next few months, at least.' Jade had only just moved in over the last few days, and she was still getting used to it herself. She glanced at the ivy-covered cottage and tried to see it through his eyes. The afternoon sun was warm and bright, its rays highlighting the yellow Cotswold stone where it peeped through the covering of ivy.

'I know it might seem a bit strange to begin with, but this is going to be your home for a while. Try to remember the name of the street and the house number… Sweetbriar Cottage, Number three, Meadow Lane.' It shouldn't be too difficult for them to do that—in fact, they were fairly isolated out here, with only one or two buildings spread out along the country road.

Connor dutifully muttered the words to himself and she gave a wry hint of a smile. That had been her mother's mantra when she had been a little girl—always remember where you live, in case you get lost and have to ask a policeman for help.

She didn't share her thoughts with the children, though. They had been through enough already this afternoon, and she wasn't going to be the one to pile any more uncertainties on their heads.

A brief flicker of pain shot through her as the worries came flooding back. Things had to work out—she couldn't bear it if anything more went wrong. As to how she was going to manage these next few weeks, taking on the care of two young children—it was a daunting task. She pulled in a deep breath. She would make it work. She had to.

'It's not very big, is it?' Rebeccah said doubtfully, and Jade looked down at her. At five years old, she was a pretty little girl, with brown hair that fell in a sleek line to her shoulders and grey eyes that reflected candour and the wide-eyed innocence of youth. She looked like a smaller version of her mother.

'No, but it's bigger than it looks inside, and at least you'll be able to have a bedroom each.'

'Who lives there?' Connor pointed towards the house next door. He, too, had his mother's grey eyes, but his hair was a little fairer, as though it had been kissed by the sun. 'His house is 'normous…like a mansion. I bet he's rich as rich, richer than anyone.'

Busy unloading the boot of the car, Jade stopped to look across at the neighbouring house. Connor was right. The house was impressive, built of honey-coloured Cotswold stone, a sprawling building, with deep gabled roofs clad with stone tiles, and dormer windows, with more windows nestling under the eaves. An overhanging roof covered the entrance porch. Altogether it was a pleasing house, and the front garden complemented it perfectly. It was well stocked, with flowering trees and shrubs that were looking a little overgrown now, and she wondered how long they had been left untended.

'I don't know about that,' Jade said. 'The man that lives there is away at the moment, so the house is empty.'

'How do you know that?' Connor was frowning again, his head tipped back to look up at her.

'The agent told me…that's the man who leased me this house,' she added in explanation. He hadn't said a lot about the man next door, just that she might not see a great deal of him because he sometimes worked unsociable hours, much like herself. 'I needed somewhere to live that was close to where I'm going to be working, and he found me this little cottage.' She collected the bags and cases together and locked the boot. 'Shall we take all these things into the house?' She started to lead the way up the path, and began to open the front door.

'I think it's haunted,' Connor said in awed tones, looking back at the house next door. 'I seed a ghost up at the window. It was staring at us.' His eyes were growing larger by the minute, and his sister took advantage of his apprehension, starting to make wailing noises and bending her arms up in front of him like an apparition, backing him into a corner. Connor started to squeal.

'It wasn't a ghost. It must have been the sunlight playing tricks on you,' Jade said.

Rebeccah let her arms fall back by her sides and studied Jade. 'You're going to work at the hospital, aren't you? Is that where they took my mummy?'

'That's right.' Jade made a face as a ripple of unease ran through her. She didn't want to be reminded of Rebeccah's mother lying injured in a hospital bed. It was altogether too heart-rending. As to her work, she wasn't ready for that either. Her new post, as senior house officer in A and E, was due to start the next day, and she had been feeling nervous about it from the first. She wasn't experienced in emergency work, and it was going to be a challenge. Now, with everything that had happened, it was just one more problem to add to everything else that she had to contend with.

'Is Nanna there as well?' Connor looked troubled.

Jade nodded and ushered the children into the cottage and along the hallway towards the kitchen. She wasn't sure how to tackle this situation, and the truth was she was feeling completely out of her depth. Perhaps it was best just to let the children ask questions, and to answer them as simply as she was able.

'Can we go and see Mummy?' Rebeccah asked. 'And Nanna? Will we be able to go and see them?'

Jade put their belongings on the worktop in the kitchen and then turned to face the children. 'I hope so...when they're feeling a little bit better perhaps. The doctors and nurses are looking after your mummy and nanna as best they can. We just have to wait a little while until they start to get well again.'

She said it confidently enough, but inside she felt sick with worry. When she had last seen Rebeccah's mother, the medical team had been battling to save her life. They had been giving her intravenous fluids to keep her from going into shock, and they had been calling for the assistance of a surgeon. As to her own mother, they were still trying to find out whether she was suffering from any internal bleeding. It seemed as though the world had been turned upside down in a matter of minutes, and now Jade was left struggling to cope with the aftermath.

She went over to the fridge and brought out a bottle of milk. 'Do you want milk and biscuits? They might keep you going until I get things sorted out for tea.'

Connor nodded and came over to the table. 'Why can't Daddy come and look after us?' he said, climbing up onto a chair. 'Then we could stay at our house.'

'He's away, Connor—he's working on the oilrig out at sea. Don't you remember?' She frowned. 'It won't be so bad staying here with me, will it?'

'No...but I haven't got all my toys. I want my fire engine.'

'It's his favourite toy,' Rebeccah said knowledgeably. 'He even takes it to bed with him.' She turned to her brother and said with a sneer, 'He isn't our dad, anyway. Not our real dad...and he's hardly ever at home.'

'So? I don't care.' Connor was scowling, and Rebeccah glared at him in return. Jade wondered whether she ought to intervene.

'I think I picked up your fire engine and put it in one

of the bags,' she said. 'Why don't you two go outside and play in the garden for a while?' She sensed that they were unsettled after what had happened, and were fizzing inside like a volcano that was about to erupt. Maybe they needed to let off some steam. With them off her hands for a while, perhaps she could take the time to phone her half-brother and let him know what had happened.

The children didn't need a second bidding. They wolfed down the milk and biscuits and then they were off like a shot through the French doors and out into the wilderness that passed for a garden. Jade watched them go. Absently, she noticed that the grass needed cutting and there were weeds that needed to be pulled, but for the time being other things had to take priority.

She went over to the phone and dialled her brother's number, aware of a hollow feeling in her stomach as she waited for the call to be put through. She could see the children through the glass doors, and she frowned when Connor came back into the kitchen and began to rummage through the bags on the worktop. Belongings were scattered far and wide until he found what he was looking for.

He looked at her in triumph. 'Got my fire engine,' he said, and ran outside once more.

Sounds of squabbling came from the garden, but just then her brother's boss answered the phone and she tried to ignore what was going on outside for a while. 'I need to talk to Ben,' she told him. 'Is he able to come to the phone? Something's happened that he needs to know about.'

'He was diving earlier today, checking the pipelines,' the boss said. 'Right now he's undergoing decompression—is there anything I can do for you?'

'There's been an accident,' she told him, 'and his wife and our mother are in hospital. I was hoping that he would be able to come home.'

'I'm so sorry. Of course I'll let him know. How are they? Is it bad?'

Jade was watching the children as she spoke, and she saw that Connor had started to climb onto the shed roof, with Rebeccah close on his heels. Her stomach knotted. It was a lean-to shed, positioned up against the fence that separated their property from the one next door. She guessed that they were trying to get a better look at the tree in the next garden. Its branches overhung the shed a little, and it was probably a big temptation to them. The children looked safe enough for the moment, but she would have to go and get them down from there.

She said, 'I don't know all the details yet. They're still doing tests at the hospital.' She pulled in a shaky breath. 'They were out on a shopping trip, and as they were crossing the road a car jumped the lights and hit them. My brother's wife has a suspected pelvic fracture and head injury, and our mother is being treated for a shoulder fracture and abdominal trauma. We don't know the full extent of their injuries yet.'

'I'm dreadfully sorry,' he said. 'I'll certainly get the message to Ben, and we'll make sure that he'll get back to you as soon as we can manage it. It might take some time—he'll be in the decompression chamber for another day or so, and then we have to wait until conditions are right to fly him home. The weather isn't always in our favour out here, but we'll send him back to you as soon as is humanly possible.'

'Thank you.' She cut the call, and sat for a moment staring bleakly into space. She had desperately wanted to talk to Ben. He was her one point of contact, and now that had been denied her she felt devastated. It was as though she was totally alone in the world, and memories poured in, washing over her like a tidal wave…recollections of a bleak childhood spent waiting for a father who never came.

Shouts from the garden drew her back to the present. There was a cracking sound as a tree branch broke, but she could see that the children were safe. Hurrying out through the French doors, she went over to the shed to see what the fuss was about. 'Come down from there,' she said.

'I seed the ghost,' Connor shrieked. 'He's coming to get us.'

Rebeccah was pale. 'I heard him,' she said in a trembling voice. 'He's got a big deep voice, and he said he wants to talk to us.'

Jade frowned as she helped the children down. She had no idea what had upset them, but it was clear that they were both shaken. She looked around but there was no sign of anyone but the three of them. 'There aren't any ghosts,' she said.

'Is, too,' Connor insisted. 'We wasn't being naughty. We was just trying to look at the tree.'

Jade turned her attention to Rebeccah, and Connor disappeared round the side of the shed. She thought that maybe he was trying to hide, but then she heard him scrabbling about. As she went to investigate what he was up to, a voice caught her unawares.

'Could I speak to you for a moment?'

Jade turned to see where the sound was coming from, putting a hand up to her temple, brushing back her shoulder-length golden curls and shielding her eyes from the sun. The children were right. It was a deep, male voice, and she was pretty sure that it didn't belong to any spectre.

The children weren't hanging around to find out who it was, but took to their heels and fled into the house. Jade glanced after them. Connor was carrying something, but she couldn't make out what it was, and at the moment she was more interested in finding out who the voice belonged to.

'I'm over here, by the gate,' the man said, and she turned to where the large wrought-iron side gate separated the back garden from the front of the house.

The sight of the man standing there gave her something of a jolt. He was tall, over six feet, with broad shoulders and lean hips, and he was dressed in a dark grey suit that screamed of expensive tailoring. He was also incredibly good-looking, with night-black hair and startlingly blue eyes.

Her heart had begun to thump discordantly but she wasn't at all sure why he was having this effect on her. It was probably more to do with the shock of seeing him standing there than with anything else.

'What do you want?' she asked, dry-mouthed. 'You've just given the children the fright of their lives. It's a wonder they didn't fall off the roof.'

'That's exactly what I wanted to talk to you about,' he said. 'I really don't think it's a good idea for you to be letting them loose like that. They're very young. Anything could have happened. They might have hurt themselves.'

'I realise that. I was watching them.'

He raised a dark brow. 'Were you? I don't think you were making a very good job of it. They shouldn't have been up there in the first place, but from what I could see they were out here on their own for several minutes before you decided to do anything about it.'

'Yes, well—at least they didn't come to any harm, and there's no damage done in the end, so I think it probably best if we just forget about it for now. Thank you for your concern, but I'll handle things from here on.' She used a dismissive tone and hoped that would be the end of it, but he wasn't about to be fobbed off.

'I'd like to come round and talk to you,' he said.

She shook her head. 'I don't think so.' At that moment she was thankful that there was a sturdy padlock on the gate. 'I've no idea who you are, and I'm certainly not inviting you around here after you've just scared the living daylights out of the children.'

He gave a faint grimace. 'I didn't mean to do that. They took fright as soon as they saw me.'

'I'm not surprised. You're not supposed to be there. The owner of the house is away, and for all I know you could be a burglar.' She had to admit that she had never seen a burglar dressed in a suit before now, but anything was possible.

'I *am* the owner,' he said. 'I've been away on a course, but I arrived back just a short time ago.'

'Anyone could say that,' Jade said. 'The agent assured me that the owner would be away for another fortnight at least.'

'There was a change of plan.' He studied her. 'Perhaps it would help if you take a look at my driving licence. Would that satisfy you as to my identity?' There was a thread of sarcasm in his voice, and he probably expected her to refuse the offer, but Jade wasn't giving in to intimidation of any sort.

'It might,' she said.

He reached into his jacket pocket and took out a thin wallet, handing it to her through the wrought-iron bars of the gate. She read the name on his licence—Callum Beresford—and winced. It was the name the agent had mentioned to her. She handed the wallet back to him.

'I had to make sure,' she said. 'I hope you understand my concerns.'

'I do.' His mouth made an odd shape, his expression halfway between cynicism and a grimace. 'Perhaps I should even be grateful for your vigilance.' He frowned. 'I'll go around to the front of the house, shall I? I really think we should talk some more.'

Jade guessed that it would be less than neighbourly to refuse his request. After all, he had at least been concerned for the children's welfare. She hesitated for a moment, and then nodded. 'All right, give me a minute, and I'll let you in.'

She started to walk back to the house. She wasn't looking forward to prolonging the conversation with him, and she wasn't at all sure what awaited her as far as the children were concerned. Given everything that had gone on today, they were totally wound up and she was dreading to discover what they might be getting up to next.

Going into the kitchen, she saw that they were bent over something on the floor. Connor was busily pouring milk into a saucer, spilling most of it in the process, and she frowned, wondering what was going on.

'We found a kitten in the garden,' he said, looking up at her. 'He's hungry. We're going to give him some milk.'

Jade glanced around and caught sight of a pathetic-looking little black kitten that was staring at them with large eyes and trying unsuccessfully to blend in with the kitchen units. She gave herself a mental shake, and didn't even think of making an issue of it. By now, she was just thankful that they were both over their fright and she was busy trying to work out how she was going to get along with her new neighbour. They hadn't had the best of beginnings.

She opened the front door to Callum Beresford and stood back to let him into the hallway. He made an imposing figure on her doorstep and she was more than a touch wary of him. His blue eyes studied her assessingly and seemed to miss nothing.

'We're in the kitchen,' she murmured, waving him through. 'You'll have to excuse the mess. We've not long arrived home.'

He walked ahead of her as she indicated, and stopped at the doorway into the room, looking in on the scene of devastation in there. Standing beside him, Jade's heart sank. It was worse than she remembered. There were toys strewn all along the worktops where Connor had abandoned them, and the rest of the bags were where she had left them when they had first come in. Added to that, there were puddles of milk all over the floor, though the kitten was doing his very best to lick them up.

Callum's features were impassive. She had absolutely no idea what he was thinking. He probably had her down as the worst housekeeper in the Cotswolds.

The children stared up at him, open-mouthed. Connor was the first to recover, and looked up at him, his eyes dark with suspicion. 'Who are you?' he said.

'I'm the man who lives next door,' Callum answered.

'In the big house?' Rebeccah asked.

'That's right.'

'No one lives there,' Connor said doubtfully, still giving him that mistrustful look. 'Is you a ghost?'

'I don't think so. At least, I wasn't the last time I looked in the mirror,' Callum answered, straight-faced. Seeing the children's worried expressions, he quickly added, 'No, I'm not. I've been away from home for a while, but now I've come back.'

Connor was clearly still unconvinced, and Jade said, 'This is the man who was trying to talk to you in the garden. He's not cross with you, and there's no need for you to be frightened.' She hoped that was true. She glanced at her neighbour, her expression willing him to agree with her.

'That's right,' he murmured, but when he looked back at her niece and nephew his expression was serious, and Jade began to wonder whether he had ever had much contact with children. These two were a handful, to be sure, but his manner with them was verging on cool. 'I do want a word with you, though,' he said. 'I think you have something of mine, don't you? I would like to have it back.'

Jade stared at him. 'I don't understand. I didn't see them take anything.'

His gaze flicked over her, skimming her jeans-clad figure and taking in the snug fit of her cotton top. 'Per-haps that's because you weren't taking too much notice of what they were getting up to.' He kept his voice low, but his tone was curt, condemning, and her mouth quivered slightly at the unfair criticism.

He turned back to the children. 'When you leaned over to look at the tree, I think one of the branches broke off, didn't it? Did you pick up the little birdhouse and feeder that was attached to the branch? It's important to me. It belonged to someone who was in my family, and I wouldn't like to lose it.'

Connor gave him a sombre look, but said nothing, and Jade guessed that he was too overwhelmed by the presence of this tall stranger to admit to anything. Rebeccah, wanting to do the right thing, spoke up for both of them. 'We didn't mean to take it. We just wanted to look at it.'

'Do you still have it? It belonged to my grandparents, and it's very precious to me. I would like to have it back.'

Jade decided that it was time to take control of the situation. 'I'm sorry about this,' she told him. 'I had no idea that this happened, but I'm sure they meant no harm. They're a little over-excited today.'

'Yes,' he said in a dour tone, 'I gathered that.'

She ignored the implied censure. Glancing at Connor, she said, 'Do you know where the birdhouse is?'

He nodded solemnly.

'Then go and fetch it for me, please.'

He did as he was told, but hesitated before handing over the bird box. He held onto the branch from the tree, looking up at Jade. 'Can I keep the stick?' he said. 'It's a well good whacker.'

Stifling a smile, she said, 'That's up to Mr Beresford,

I think.' She sent her new neighbour a quick glance. 'What do you think?'

He looked at the boy. 'I imagine that will be all right,' he said, 'as long as you promise that you won't go breaking anything with it. I don't want to look out from my house and find that you've smashed a window or broken down the plants in the garden.'

'It's not up to you,' Connor said. 'We live here. It's not your garden.'

Callum made a wry face. 'Actually, it is, in a way. I'm your landlord. Do you know what that means?'

Connor shook his head, giving him an uncertain look.

'It means that the house belongs to me, but I'm letting you live in it for a while. I want you to enjoy staying here, but there's to be no more climbing on the shed. It's dangerous, and you could hurt yourself. Do we understand each other?'

Connor nodded.

'Good. Then perhaps we can be friends.'

Connor clearly wasn't so sure about that. It was something he would have to think about. Giving the stranger a look from under his lashes, he sidled away, putting the stick in a safe place in a gap between the side of the fridge and the kitchen wall. He probably thought Callum wouldn't bother trying to remove it from there.

Going over to the kitten, Connor coaxed it up into his arms. Then he stood and watched the man from a corner of the room, silently weighing him up, until Rebeccah whispered to him and led him outside.

Jade studied her new neighbour. 'I didn't realise that you owned both properties,' she said. 'I hope that's not going to be a problem while I'm living here. I prefer to deal with the children in my own way, and if you have any issues with them I would rather you spoke to me about them than to them.'

He nodded. 'That's fair enough. At least now we both know where we stand.' He picked up the bird-house and feeder. 'I'm glad that we've had the chance to talk,' he said, 'but I should go now. I have a lot of things to be getting on with.'

She nodded and started to move towards the hallway.

'You don't need to trouble yourself,' he said. 'I'll see myself out.' He glanced towards the garden. 'I expect you'll want to go and keep an eye on the children.'

'They'll be fine,' she murmured. She went to the front door. Opening it, she said, 'I'm sorry that we had such a bad start, but I'm sure you won't have any cause for complaint from now on.' She fervently hoped that was true. The last thing she needed was to be embroiled in a battle with her landlord.

He gave a brief smile. 'I'm sure we'll get along just fine.'

As soon as he had gone, she went back to the kitchen. The children were playing with the kitten on the lawn, and she watched them, thinking about her mother and her sister-in-law, and feeling sad inside for everything that had happened. She was all that the children had for the moment, and she would do all in her power to see that they were safe and happy.

Picking up the phone, she called the hospital and asked for news. The encounter with Callum Beresford had unsettled her, but she had to let it go. She had enough problems on her plate, without worrying about

her dealings with her aloof, unsociable neighbour. She
would try to put him out of her thoughts, and with any
luck they would be able to avoid running into each
other for the foreseeable future.

CHAPTER TWO

'CONNOR—put the kitten down and start getting dressed for school, please. We need to hurry up.' Jade was becoming increasingly anxious about the way time was slipping away from her. Looking after children was an entirely new thing for her, an undertaking that was strewn with pitfalls, and so far, no matter how efficiently she had tried to organise things, nothing seemed to be going right.

Added to that, she was supposed to make a start in A and E that morning and she was desperate for everything to go well. It wouldn't do to be late on her first day, would it? Despite her nervousness, she wanted to make a good impression.

She recalled the first meeting with her new boss— at her interview just a short time ago—when she had quickly learned to respect him for his obvious skill and experience. Mr Ramsay, the consultant, was an older man, in his fifties, she guessed, a kindly, thoughtful man, and she didn't want to let him down. They had got on well together, and she felt that he would be supportive, but it was still up to her to give of her best.

'As soon as you're both dressed, I want you to go downstairs and get your breakfast. I put some cereal out in your bowls but then I found out that there's not enough milk, so you'll have to leave those and eat the toast I've made for you instead.' She hadn't realised that Connor had been busy filling up the kitten's saucer at regular intervals, and it was too late now to go and get fresh milk.

'Can we keep the kitten?' Rebeccah asked, picking it up as it escaped Connor's clutches.

'I don't know.' Jade made a face. 'I know how much you both like him, but we don't know where he's come from. We'll keep him for now, to make sure that he's safe, but I'll have to put some notices out to see if someone's looking for him. He might belong to another family.'

Rebeccah wasn't deterred. 'But if no one comes for him, he might get to stay with us for always,' she said, smiling happily.

'Perhaps, but don't get your hopes up too much. His real family might be missing him.' She glanced at Rebeccah, who was nearly dressed. 'You're doing very well,' she said. 'I want to go and have a quick shower— I'll be five minutes, that's all. Will you take Connor downstairs and make sure he gets his breakfast? I should be down before you've finished.'

Rebeccah nodded, looking older and wiser than her tender years. 'Mummy always asks me to help get Connor ready. He's not very good, you know. He takes ages to get his clothes on because he always stops to play with his toys.'

Jade made a wry smile. 'I'd noticed that.' She made

sure that the children had finished getting dressed, and then went to the bathroom. Ideally, she wanted to sit down with the children and have breakfast with them, but things were running away from her this morning. Instead, she took the quickest shower she'd ever had and then hurried downstairs. To her relief, she found that the children were sitting at the kitchen table, munching away at their toast and also at their breakfast cereal.

'Are you fetching us from school today?' Connor asked. He looked up at her, his mouth smeared with a creamy white covering of milk, and Jade frowned, wondering where that had come from.

'No, your mummy's friend, Libby, is going to meet you when school finishes, and she said that she'll look after you until I come home from work. You'll be able to play with her children, won't you? I expect you'll like that.'

They both nodded. 'We sometimes go to Libby's for tea.' Rebeccah's expression became serious. 'When will Mummy and Nanna be coming home?'

'I'm not sure,' Jade told her. 'I talked to the doctor on the telephone a little while ago, and he said that he's doing everything he can to make them feel better. I'm going to see them at the hospital today, and I'll let you know how they are when I come home. I'll give them a kiss from both of you, shall I?'

'Yes,' Rebeccah said, and Connor began blowing kisses across his palm. Jade watched the children for a moment then glanced at their breakfast bowls. Their cereal was already half-eaten, and that struck her as odd. Scanning the table, she saw that there was a white jug in the centre, filled to the brim with milk.

'Where did that come from?' she asked. 'There
wasn't any milk left in the fridge.' Her brows met in a
furrowed line. Come to that, she didn't even recognise
the jug.

'We got it from the man next door,' Connor told her.

Jade stared at him. 'I don't understand. Are you saying that you went round and asked him for a jug of
milk?'

'Yes, we both did.'

She blinked, trying to take that in. Surely they
hadn't? 'How could that be? I thought you were afraid
of him. How did you pluck up the courage to do that?'

'I wanted my breakfast,' Connor said in a matter-of-
fact tone, as though he was amazed that she still didn't
get the full picture. 'I didn't want toast. I always have
wheaty flakes for my breakfast, so I took my bowl
round and asked him to put some milk on them.'

Jade felt a wave of heat rise up inside her and flood
her cheeks. Was it possible for her to be humiliated any
more? Could the floor open and swallow her up?

'I think he felt sorry for us,' Rebeccah piped up, 'be-
cause he went and fetched a jug and filled it up for
us. He said, "Are you two getting enough to eat?" and
Connor said, "Well, sometimes we don't get no tea if
Mummy's too busy." And the man said, "Oh dear," and
I said, "But we might have a take-away instead."'

Jade closed her eyes and groaned inwardly, the wave
turning to a tide of embarrassment that surged through
her. What must her neighbour have thought when these
two little waifs and strays had appeared on his doorstep,
holding out their cereal bowls and pleading for sustenance? It didn't bear thinking about. If he believed she

was their mother he probably had her marked down as a serious candidate for neglect of her responsibilities, given their previous encounter.

There was no time to remedy the situation right now, though. 'I think you should leave it to me to sort out the milk situation next time,' she said. Jade braced herself. 'Now, we need to get a move on. We have to leave here in a few minutes, so I want you to hurry up and finish your breakfast and then we must get in the car and set off for school.'

Thankfully, she didn't run into her new neighbour as they left the house. She wasn't ready to face him, and she certainly hadn't the wherewithal for a confrontation with him just now. There were enough butterflies in her stomach already at the thought of starting work in A and E. It was one of the most demanding specialties and, being relatively inexperienced in emergency work, she would need all the help she could get.

As it was, things turned out quite differently to what she was expecting when she arrived at the hospital. Instead of a gentle easing in and a helping hand from one of the nurses to show her where everything was, she found herself being plunged straight into chaos.

'I don't have time to talk now,' the triage nurse said, pushing a hand through her chestnut-coloured hair. 'We're run off our feet. There was an accident at one of the factories in town, and we've multiple casualties to deal with. Dr Franklin is co-ordinating everything, and you'll just have to pitch in as best you can. There's a man being brought in by ambulance—a suspected heart attack. He should be here in about ten minutes. Perhaps you can take the lead with that one.'

'Yes, of course.' Jade hoped that she was up to it. Glancing around, she asked, 'Where is the consultant… Mr Ramsay? I haven't seen him around anywhere.'

'No—you won't be seeing him.' The nurse frowned. 'He was taken ill—but you wouldn't have heard about that, would you? He was away on holiday for a few days and went down with some sort of food poisoning. It's affected his kidneys, and now he's being treated in the renal unit. For a while it was touch and go as to whether he would pull through.'

Jade was shocked. 'I'm so sorry. I had no idea. I hope he'll be all right.'

'So do I. We all think the world of him. As it is, he's going to be laid up for some time, from the sound of things. That is bad enough, from his point of view, but it's left us all in a state of upheaval here.' The nurse managed an apologetic smile. 'Look, I have to go. I'm supposed to be helping out with a multiple fracture. I'm Katie, by the way. If you need any help, just yell.'

Jade winced. Everyone was snowed under, and she doubted if anyone would be able to spare the time to spoonfeed a new senior house officer. She was being thrown in at the deep end, and she guessed it was a case of swim or go under.

Katie hurried away, and Jade decided that maybe the best way for her to prepare for the incoming patient would be to find out where everything was kept, so that she could lay her hands on whatever it was that she might need. She went and collared a nurse who was fetching supplies, and showered her with questions.

'Blood and lab forms are in boxes behind the reception desk,' the girl said. 'Medications are next to the

A and E makeshift laboratory, and other supplies are in the room opposite the doctors' lounge. If you need anything else, ask Dr Franklin, the registrar, or James in Reception.' The nurse hurried away, leaving Jade floundering.

'But surely, I need a key for the drugs cupboard?' she called after her, but she was too late. The nurse had disappeared round a corner.

'Is there a problem here?'

Jade froze at the sound of that voice. It couldn't be, could it? A prickle of tension ran along her spine. There was no getting away from it…the deep, gravelled tones were somehow disturbingly familiar. Turning around slowly, she looked up at the owner of the voice and immediately felt as though the stuffing had been knocked out of her.

'What are you doing here?' The words were dredged up from inside her, shock draining the blood from her face as she took in the sight of Callum Beresford's long, lean frame.

'I could ask you the same question.' His glance moved over her, taking in the white doctor's jacket that she wore over smoothly fitting black trousers and cotton top. He looked as though he was almost as stunned as she was.

She lifted her chin. 'I work here, as of today. I'm the new senior house officer—Dr Holbrook.'

He shook his head. 'No, surely not? That can't be… Fate wouldn't be so unkind, would it? I was expecting someone sensible and efficient, someone who would be in control of the situation…a doctor that I could rely on to be on top form.'

Her shoulders stiffened. 'What makes you think that I'm not all of those things?'

His mouth made a wry slant. 'We've met before, remember? I imagine you have a full-time job looking after those two wayward children. I would have thought that they would be more than enough to keep you occupied and at home.' He laid a slight emphasis on that last word.

She lifted a brow. 'Are you seriously suggesting that a woman's place is in the home, by the kitchen sink, surrounded by young children?' She frowned and shook her head. 'If so, I have to tell you that isn't always the case these days.'

He studied her broodingly. 'Yes, I realise that. In some instances it seems that's an unfortunate fact.'

She stared at him, about to make a pithy comment in reply, but then a siren sounded in the distance, and she said, 'I have a patient coming in, and I need to get ready for him. Do you know where I can get a key to the drugs cupboard?'

'I'll sort one out for you, just as soon as we've checked your details. I've been busy transferring patients to Theatre or I would have dealt with this earlier.' He made a brief grimace. 'You had better come with me.'

'My patient?' she queried. 'I was supposed to be looking after a heart-attack patient.'

'I'll get Dr Franklin to supervise that one.'

He turned away and she hurried after him. 'It's all very well you giving me orders,' she said on a terse note. 'I don't even know who you are—or what your position is here.'

'I'm the acting consultant while Mr Ramsay is away. I was brought in to take over from him.'

She winced. She might have known. He certainly looked the part. He was wearing another immaculate grey suit, which sat well on his tall, firmly muscled frame, and he appeared to be every inch the consultant, an authoritative, confident man, totally in command. Her spirits sank.

He stared at her. 'If what you say is correct, I'm afraid it looks very much as though you and I are going to be working together for some time. Perhaps we had both better get used to the idea.'

He wasn't taking any chances, though. It was only after he had verified that she really was supposed to be there that he reluctantly allowed her to go and start work. As she moved away from him and went in search of her patient, she felt his gaze searing into her back and she had the feeling that he was going to be watching her like a hawk.

She tried to put him out of her mind and hurried to meet the ambulance crew as they wheeled in a little boy on a trolley.

'This is Dean Matthews,' the paramedic said, bringing the trolley to a halt in a side bay. 'He's four years old, suspected poisoning from beta-blockers—propranolol. Apparently he took some pills out of his grandmother's bag. We have the bottle, and it's almost empty.'

Jade was worried. The child looked very ill, and she knew that a propranolol overdose could be fatal. 'Do we know how many he took?'

The paramedic shook his head. 'No, but there should have been a fair few in the bottle, and the family think he must have taken them well over an hour ago. His heart rate has fallen dramatically and he's hypotensive. We've been monitoring his cardiac output on the way here.'

'It doesn't look good, does it?' Jade said in an undertone. She signalled for a nurse to come and help. 'I'm going to get him on activated charcoal right away.' She worked quickly, hoping that the charcoal would help to remove any of the drug that hadn't already been absorbed into his bloodstream. The boy was being given oxygen through a mask, and her main concern was that the drug had reduced the activity of his heart to an extent where it could damage his organ systems. Her priority was to restore perfusion to those systems.

'Thanks,' she told the young paramedic, who had hung around to await results. She could see that he was worried. 'We'll take over from here. Do you want me to let you know how he gets on?'

He nodded. 'Please. I've another call coming in, but I would like to know what happens here.'

'Of course. I'll update you when you come in again.'

'Thank you. I'm Sam, by the way.'

'OK, Sam.' She acknowledged him briefly, and with that he went away. With the nurse's help, Jade wheeled the child into an available treatment room and made sure that he was hooked up to the monitors. Just as they settled him, though, the little boy started to convulse, and a few seconds later he lost consciousness.

'I'm not getting a pulse,' Jade said anxiously. 'He's gone into cardiac arrest.' She worked as fast as she was able to put in an endotracheal airway, and then started chest compressions with the palm of her hand, while the nurse took over with the oxygen.

Jade was desperately afraid that her efforts were to no avail, but after a while the nurse glanced at the monitor and said, 'He's back with us.'

Jade was relieved, but she was still feeling apprehensive. The child's cardiac output was thready, and she swiftly established an intravenous line and gave the child atropine.

It didn't appear to be having much effect. 'Helen,' she said, "we'll start him on the charcoal. You'll need to watch him in case of vomiting.'

The nurse nodded. 'What about blood tests?'

'I want U and E and blood glucose, a complete blood count and a toxicology screen. We'll monitor him for pulse, blood pressure and perfusion.'

'OK.'

A woman came into the treatment room and clutched at Jade's arm. 'What's happening to my little boy? Nobody's telling me anything. He's just lying there. Can you do something to help him?'

'We're doing everything that we can,' she told the woman, using a soothing tone. 'He's absorbed a lot of his grandmother's medication, and that has had the effect of slowing down his heart and causing a collapse of his vital functions. We're working to restore his heart and circulation.'

'But he'll be all right, won't he?'

'I hope so,' Jade said gently. 'We'll need to admit him for observation, so that we can monitor his condition over the next few hours.'

The woman was near to tears. 'We had no idea that

he'd been searching in his grandmother's bag. It was up on a high cupboard, and we didn't think he could reach that far. Then we found out that he had pulled up a chair, and climbed on to it. He thought his grandmother had some sweets for him.'

Jade was sympathetic. 'I know that it can be hard to watch children every minute,' she said. 'He's at an age, though, where he's likely to be into everything, and you need to make sure that any tablets and medicines are locked away securely.'

'I will. I won't ever let this happen again…if only you can save him…' She sent Jade a pleading look. 'I want to stay with him.'

Jade nodded. 'That's all right. He seems to be stable for the moment, and the nurse will be here to answer any questions that you might have. I have to go and see to my other patients, but I'll come back and check on him in a few minutes.'

She was glad that the child's mother was by his side. Seeing them together made her think of her own mother, lying ill in a hospital bed, and a feeling of sadness overwhelmed her. She had been trying so hard to keep going, to do everything that was necessary, but all the time she was struggling with the knowledge that people she loved were fighting major battles of their own. Just as soon as she had the opportunity, she was going to look in on them. She needed to know that her mother and sister-in-law were going to be all right.

'How is the child?' Callum was waiting for her as she left the treatment room. He was looking over the boy's chart, and she wondered if he was checking to see if there was anything that she had omitted to do.

'It's too early to say, just yet. His condition has sta-
bilised for the moment, but he isn't out of danger just
yet. Helen is monitoring him.'

'All right. Perhaps you could go and look at the patient in treatment room four. He appears to have trod-
den on a nail.' He handed her the chart, his hand
brushing hers, and a shower of invisible electric sparks
shot along the length of her arm, confusing her and
rooting her to the spot.

He seemed to hesitate momentarily, and she hardly
dared look at him in case he had registered her sudden
tension. Perhaps he was waiting for an answer, but her
voice seemed to be stuck in her throat. Instead, she simply nodded.

He moved away from her, and she hoped that would
be the end of it, but for the rest of the morning she had
the nagging feeling that he was keeping an eye on her.
He never made it too obvious, but she was aware that
he was checking up on her, either by glancing through
the tests she had ordered or by inspecting her notes and
scrutinising the medications she had prescribed.

By the time her lunch-break came along, she was
glad to get away. It was one thing to be supervised, but
it was quite another to be under constant surveillance
as though he expected her to make some dreadful mistake at any minute.

Keyed up, and thoroughly on edge, she went up to
the ward where her mother was being cared for. Her
mother was lying propped up in bed, looking frail and
lost, her fair hair falling in soft tendrils against her
cheeks. Jade could see that her left arm was in a sling.

Jade gave her a gentle hug. 'I can't believe this has

happened,' she said, 'but I'm so glad that you're at least sitting up and able to talk to me.'

'It was all a bit of a shock,' her mother said. 'I thought I'd just fractured my shoulder, but then I started to feel really ill and they all started to rush about doing tests and things. They said that I was bleeding inside, and they didn't know what was causing it, but in the end they had to send me to Theatre for an operation. I feel much better now, but I'm a bit sore.'

'I expect you will be for a while,' Jade said. 'I had a word with the doctor. He said that they found a small tear in your liver, but they managed to stitch it up. As long as you rest, you should be all right, but they're going to keep you in here for a few days, just to make sure.'

Her mother looked at her, her green eyes troubled. 'How are you coping? You're looking after the children, aren't you? Is everything working out all right? How are they bearing up?'

'Everything is fine,' Jade said. 'Don't worry yourself. The children are worried, obviously, but they seem to be taking it all in their stride. Rebeccah is older, so she seems to have more of an inkling about what's going on, but she's coping. They were both hoping that Ben would come home, but he's still in the decompression chamber. I should think he'll be here as soon as he's able.'

'That will make Gemma feel better, I expect.' Her mother frowned. 'How is she?'

'I'm not absolutely sure, but I'm going to see her in a few minutes. As far as I know, they've managed to stabilise her pelvis in Theatre. She's lost a lot of blood, though.'

They talked for a while longer, and then Jade gave her mother a kiss and stood up, ready to go. 'I brought you some magazines,' she said. 'I'll hunt out a few more for you and bring them along tomorrow. You take care now, and get some rest.'

Her mother smiled. 'You're an angel. You always were able to cope, no matter what life threw at you. You always seemed so strong. Look at how you looked after your brother when he was little—I feel so guilty sometimes because of the way I failed you back then, and here you are, going through a similar situation all over again.' She sent Jade a pensive look. 'I know this can't be easy for you, and you must have a lot to contend with just now. You should try to take some time out for yourself.'

'I will.' Jade didn't think there was much chance of that, but it would make her mother happy to think all was going well.

'You were going to start your new job today, weren't you? Is everything working out all right?'

'Yes, it's turning out just fine,' Jade lied. She wasn't going to burden her mother with her problems. 'At least it means I'm on hand to come up and visit you whenever I get the opportunity.'

She left the room a minute or so later and went in search of Gemma, her half-brother's wife. Gemma's condition was much worse than her mother's, and Jade was shocked when she saw her. The accident and the haemorrhage that followed had taken their toll on her.

Her sister-in-law was almost as white as the bandages that held the dressing in place on her head, and the brown of her hair made a stark contrast to her pale skin.

She seemed very weak and tired, and Jade guessed that she was in quite a lot of pain and discomfort.

Even so, Gemma wanted to know about the children. 'Are they all right? Have they settled in with you?'

'Yes. They're doing just fine, and they send their love. I told them that you'll be staying here for a little while, but that they could come and see you as soon as you were feeling stronger. The doctors don't think it would be a good idea for them to come in just yet.'

'I know.' Gemma was near to tears. 'Thanks for taking care of them for me. I was hoping that Ben would bring them to me, but I expect he's still out on the rig. He spends more time there than he does with us, but perhaps that's how he wants it. Sometimes I wonder if we made a mistake, getting married.'

Jade reached out and touched her hand. 'You mustn't think like that. Ben loves you.'

'I don't think so—not enough, anyway. Why else would he spend so much time away from us? And I don't think he cares about the children—why should he after all? They're not his, so I suppose he can't be expected to love them the way I do.' Her voice faded.

'I'm sure you have it all wrong,' Jade said. 'He loves all of you, and he'll be here just as soon as he can manage it. The last I heard, he was still in the decompression chamber.'

'Maybe.' She could see that Gemma wasn't convinced. 'It takes something like this to make you take stock of things and realise what's important in life. At least I have the children.'

'You have Ben, and me and Mum as well,' Jade told her. 'You're not alone. You mustn't think like that.'

Jade stayed with Gemma until her sister-in-law's mood had lifted a little. She knew something of what Gemma was going through…she was feeling lost and alone. Her own childhood experiences had left her feeling much the same way, making her reluctant to believe that she could rely on anyone.

Her lunch-break came to an end and she hurried back to A and E. The little boy who had taken the propranolol was showing signs of recovery, and she was pleased about that. She checked him over, and left the treatment room feeling glad that at least something was going right.

'He was fortunate,' Callum said, coming over to sign her chart and allow her to pass the boy over to admissions. 'If his family had left it much longer before they realised what he had done, things could have been far worse.'

She nodded. 'It's easy to be wise after the event, I suppose. Children will always get up to mischief of some sort, but I expect his family will keep medicines securely locked away from now on.'

He gave her a long look, those blue eyes lancing into her. 'I imagine that's something you know a lot about—the mischief, I mean.'

She managed a hollow smile. 'That reminds me—about this morning,' she began. 'I didn't know that the children had come to you, asking for milk. I was in the shower, and I didn't realise that they had left the house.'

'I guessed as much, and it sort of went along with what I've come to expect. You don't have to explain.'

'No…but I want to. You see, under normal circumstances I would have had enough milk to keep us going, but then we took in a stray kitten, and he seems to have guzzled all I had.'

'I noticed him yesterday. As for your breakfast problems, I take it that your husband is no good at helping out in that kind of situation? I'd have thought that with two of you in the house, one or other of you could manage to keep an eye on things.'

'I'm not married,' she told him.

'Ah…I see.'

'I don't think you do.'

She was about to explain the situation to him, but before she could get her act together he said, 'Well, let's just say that it all makes some kind of sense now. No wonder you're struggling, if you're on your own.'

He gave her an assessing glance, and then added, 'I'm afraid I didn't really have time to say very much to the children this morning—I planned on getting into work early, and they caught me on the hop, so to speak.'

She frowned. 'I'm sorry that they came and disturbed you. They shouldn't have done that.'

'It's not a problem,' he said. 'I realise that you're having trouble keeping it all together, but I guess you're not alone. A lot of single parents seem to find it difficult to manage.'

He signed her chart while she was still staring at him open-mouthed, and he didn't give her the opportunity to set things straight. He didn't stay around to talk any longer, but strode away to treat a patient who was being rushed into the emergency room.

Jade was kept busy for the rest of the afternoon. She was a bit out of her depth, but she tried to get by without asking for help as far as she was able, because she didn't want to give Callum any more reasons for regretting that she was on his team.

Despite her anxieties, for the most part things went well. She even managed to have a laugh with the paramedic, Sam, who came in to see how little Dean was doing.

'Hi,' he said, coming across the room to her just as she finished a coffee-break. 'How is the little fellow? Did he pull through all right?'

She nodded. 'Yes, he's doing much better now. We're going to keep him in hospital for a day or so, but it's more of a precaution than anything else. I think he'll be fine from now on.'

'That's good.' Sam smiled, his eyes crinkling at the corners as he studied her. 'I expect we'll run into each other quite a lot if you're going to be working here from now on. It seems as though my visits to the hospital are suddenly going to be much brighter than I could have hoped for.' He looked her over. 'Things are definitely looking up. You're by far the best-looking doctor I've seen around here in a long while.'

Jade gave him an answering smile. 'And you're a smooth-tongued Casanova if ever I heard one,' she said. 'I bet you've had plenty of practice charming the girls.' He was a good-looking young man, with dark hair that fell softly over his forehead and grey eyes that were full of dancing lights.

'Not nearly as much as you'd think.' He moved a little closer to her. 'I'd really like to get to know you better. How about we take off from here when you finish work and go and get ourselves something to eat? I know a good place not too far from here.'

'Sorry, but I can't,' she said. Even if she had wanted to, there were two small reasons why assignations of any kind were out of the question right now. Rebeccah and Connor would be taking up most of her free time for the foreseeable future.

Sam frowned, but just as she thought of trying to soften the blow, a shadow came between them.

'Perhaps you two should continue your cosy little chat later,' Callum said. 'There are patients waiting to be seen.' He looked at Jade, his jaw set in a firm line. 'I think it would be a good idea if you were to go and attend to them.' Then he turned a fraction, his gaze shooting warning sparks in Sam's direction.

Sam took the warning on board and began to make a strategic exit, but he managed to mouth, 'Be seeing you,' to Jade as he went.

Jade sent Callum a guarded look. 'I was on my way back from a break,' she said. 'I don't think I was being remiss in any way. I was just about to head for the treatment room.'

'I hope you were,' he said. 'Break's over.' He moved off in the direction of the reception desk, and Jade stared after him.

She sighed inwardly. It wasn't going to be easy working with Callum Beresford, that was for sure, and the fact that he was her neighbour and landlord only served to make things doubly difficult.

Was she going to be able to find a way to get along with him? At the moment, that seemed highly unlikely.

CHAPTER THREE

'How long have you been having these headaches, Stephen?' Jade needed some clues as to what was causing her patient's problems, but so far she had little to go on. There was scant previous medical history where this man was concerned.

'They started a couple of weeks ago, but they're getting much worse. This one today is really bad. I didn't think I would make it to my GP's surgery, so I came here instead. I've been vomiting, and I still feel very nauseous.'

Jade debated with herself about what to do. She was already feeling under pressure because Callum had made it clear that he wanted a swift throughput of patients and she knew that he was still monitoring her progress from a distance, as he had the previous day. Even now, she could feel his gaze fixed on her from across the room.

She wasn't quite sure what to make of this patient, though. On the face of it, his problems could possibly be put down to migraine, but she was wary of making such a quick diagnosis and sending him on his way.

Looking at him, she could see that although he looked unwell right now, he was a generally fit man in his late thirties.

'Is there anything you've noticed that starts them off?'

'No. Nothing that I can think of.'

She examined him, checking his neurological responses and his sensitivity to light. Perhaps the fact that he was in such good shape was making her extra-cautious—after all, he wasn't in the habit of seeking medical help, and that in itself gave her reason to think that there might be something more to his case than met the eye.

'I think, Stephen, to be on the safe side, I'm going to send you for a CT scan. That might give me a more of an idea about what's going on. In the meantime, I'll give you an analgesic for the pain and something to stop you from vomiting.'

'Am I going to have the scan today? I don't want to have to keep coming back here. I really want to get this sorted out now. I have a business to run, and I can't think straight with this terrible headache. I can't afford to take time off, but I'm useless like this—I feel as though I just want to go and lie down somewhere until the pain goes away.'

'I'll send you to get it done right away, and I think it might be as well for me to get someone to go with you, just in case you feel sick again. I'll see if I can get hold of a nurse and a wheelchair.' She didn't want him to suffer from an attack of dizziness and perhaps fall, especially while he was under her care.

Jade set things in motion, and when he was on his

way she went to see to her other patients, aware that Callum was still following her progress from afar, even though he was attending to a patient of his own.

Katie passed her a chart. 'A little boy, five years old, with breathing difficulties.'

'Thanks.' Jade went to find him, and introduced herself to his mother, who was holding him on her lap.

'Let's see if we can find out what the problem is, shall we?' Jade murmured, smiling at the little boy. 'Can I listen to your chest with my stethoscope? Do you want to try it first?'

The child nodded, and listened through the earpieces, his eyes widening and a hint of a smile touching his lips. He was suffering from a chest infection, Jade discovered, and she was concerned that he might be having a problem with his ears as well. In order to check that out, she needed to take a close look at his eardrums, but when she searched in the pockets of her white jacket for her auriscope, she couldn't find it.

She grimaced, remembering that she had mislaid it earlier. Rebeccah and Connor had been helping her to tidy up her medical case last night at the cottage, and perhaps they had moved it.

She glanced at the child's mother and said, 'Will you excuse me for just a moment? Perhaps, while I'm gone, you could tell the nurse about the nature of the chest infections Taylor has suffered from before this. I think we may need to do some further investigations. I'll be back very shortly.'

She left them with Katie, instructing her to give the boy oxygen to help his breathing, and hurried over to the doctors' lounge, where she took her handbag out of her locker. There was just the faintest possibility that the children might have put the instrument in there. Just as she was rummaging through the contents of her bag, though, Callum walked into the room.

Jade turned, giving him a look of startled apprehension and he said, frowning, 'What's the matter? Have you lost something? I thought I saw you going through your medical case earlier. Didn't you find what you were looking for?'

She stared up at him distractedly. 'No, I didn't... I thought perhaps I could manage without it for a while, but things didn't turn out that way, and now I need to check in my handbag.'

He sent her a quizzical look, and she realised that she wasn't explaining herself very well. 'I thought I'd put my auriscope alongside all my other equipment,' she added, 'but it wasn't so. I seem to have mislaid it. It's very strange, because I know that I had it with me last night at home.'

He sent her a pitying look. 'Organisation isn't your strong point, is it?'

She made a face. What had she expected from him? His opinion of her hadn't been good from the outset, had it? 'Believe it or not,' she said, 'I'm usually quite good at sorting things out and knowing where to find things. I can usually put my hands on whatever I need within a moment or two.'

'Really? You amaze me,' he said, going over to the coffee-machine and filling up a mug with the hot liquid. 'Does this ability not quite stretch to things like medical equipment and breakfast times?'

She disregarded his comments while she continued

to search in her bag, and after a minute or two she exclaimed in triumph, 'Found it.' She brought out the auriscope from the depths of her handbag. 'How on earth did it get in there?'

It seemed fairly clear cut that the children had had something to do with it. They had been curious about everything while she'd been trying to sort out her medical kit. Perhaps one of them had slipped the instrument into her bag instead of putting it back in the case, where it belonged.

Then, belatedly, it dawned on her what Callum had said. She stared at him. 'What do you mean, breakfast times? What do they have to do with anything?' Was he still having a go at her about the milk episode?

He took a long swallow of his coffee. 'I guess they're just another item on the list of things that you have problems with. At least, Connor seems to think so.' She stared at him blankly and he went on, 'He was quite put out because you had forgotten to buy any more wheaty flakes, and that meant he was going to go to school hungry.'

'When did he tell you that?'

'This morning, when he came round to my house with his empty cereal bowl.' He made a faint smile. 'He wanted me to fill it up for him. He said Rebeccah wasn't too fussed about what she had to eat, but he didn't want to go without his wheaty flakes if he could help it. I gathered that he wasn't too impressed with the contents of your kitchen cupboards.' He sent her a thoughtful glance. 'I suppose your organisational skills don't extend quite as far as the weekly shop.'

She blinked, ignoring the sarcasm. 'You're surely not telling me that he came round to you again?'

He nodded. 'He certainly did. Luckily, I *had* done my weekly shop, and the cereals just happened to be on my list. He was pleased about that. It seems that I'm flavour of the month with him at the moment in that respect, but I get the impression that you're about halfway down the league table. You have some catching up to do.' There was a glint in his blue eyes as he said it.

She closed her eyes to shut out the shame. 'I'm so sorry,' she managed at last. 'I told him not to keep bothering you, but he can be a very determined young man when he wants something.'

'Perhaps it would help if you kept a closer eye on him. It's not necessarily a good thing for him to be wandering about as he pleases.'

Jade pressed her lips together. 'You're right, of course. I should have sat down with them for breakfast—I managed to sit with them for the last few minutes, but I just seem to be finding it a struggle to get it all together first thing these days.' She hesitated. 'I hope you realise that there was no way he was going to go hungry—I had plenty of other alternatives on offer.'

'I did wonder about that.'

She frowned, beginning to remember all the arguments that had gone on that morning—first about the choice of cereals, then the flavours of the jam that weren't up to expectations, and that had been without counting the squabbles she'd had to break up over who was going to play with which toy. How Gemma managed to keep a lid on things was a complete mystery to her. Jade's pot of trouble was boiling over.

'It's all come about because I've started this new job,' she said, 'and I'm having to rush about to get the children to school or to their childminder on time. I've not quite managed to get on top of things yet…' She stopped, realising that she was simply outlining all her weaknesses to him, and that would never do. She was low enough in his estimation already, without her confirming the matter.

'Anyway,' she said, 'at least I've managed to find my auriscope, and that's the most important thing right now. I really should get back to my patients.' She gave him a fleeting, uncertain glance. 'I'll have a word with Connor when I get home—I'll make sure that he doesn't come bothering you again.'

He followed her out of the room. 'He doesn't bother me. I'm just concerned that he keeps wandering around without your knowledge.'

'Yes…well, it won't happen again.'

'We'll see.'

His sceptical comment tugged at a nerve, and she walked briskly along the corridor, hoping that somehow she might manage to shake him off. She went in search of her young patient with the chest infection, and found that his problems were probably going to be relatively easy to sort out. Just as she had written out a request for a chest X-ray, though, Helen came hurrying towards her.

'Jade, your patient with the headaches is convulsing—will you come and take a look at him?' Helen's blue eyes were troubled. 'We've managed to get him on a trolley and he's been taken to the treatment room.'

'I'm on my way.' Jade walked swiftly alongside her, wondering what could have gone wrong.

'His father is with him, by the way. Apparently he

went to his son's workplace to have a word with him about something, and discovered that he was here. He's come to see what's wrong.'

Jade hurried to the treatment room and carefully examined Stephen. 'I'm going to put in an intravenous line and give him diazepam to see if that will stop the convulsions,' she told Helen. 'We'd better get a glucose measurement, along with a full blood count, clotting screen and urea and electrolytes.'

After a while Stephen's convulsions stopped but Jade was alarmed to see that he was slipping into unconsciousness. She quickly intubated him, making sure that he was getting an adequate supply of oxygen, and then she said worriedly, 'We need to put in an arterial line and a urinary catheter. I'm concerned about his hypertension—we'd better get the neurologist down here urgently to take a look at him.'

Helen nodded, and went to the phone. The man's father watched the rush of activity and came forward as Jade was looking over the results of the CT scan. 'What's happening to him? I don't understand how any of this can have come about. He was fine this morning when I spoke to him.'

Jade said quietly, 'It looks as though your son could be suffering from a brain haemorrhage. The CT scan shows an aneurysm, and it may be that it has started to leak, or it may even have burst as he was on his way back here. He needs to see a surgeon right away. I'm very sorry.'

The man shook his head. 'This is serious, isn't it?'

'Yes, I'm afraid it is.'

He shook his head. 'None of this makes any sense.

He was all right earlier this morning. They told me at his office that he seemed fine, and that he just had a bad headache and wanted to come and get some medication for it. He thought A and E would be able to deal with his problem quickly.' He stared at her, his expression full of disbelief. 'He can't be ill. He was playing squash yesterday, for heaven's sake—I just don't see how he can be all right one minute, and unconscious the next.'

'I know this is upsetting for you,' Jade said, 'but I can promise you that we're doing everything we can for him. It's most likely that he'll be going up to Theatre in a short time, and the surgeon will operate to try to stop the bleeding.'

He looked at her blankly. 'This is a nightmare.'

'I know. I'm very sorry.'

His jaw set. 'Where were you when this was happening to him? I don't understand why he was on his own in here.'

'He was never on his own,' Jade said gently. 'I can assure you that someone was with him the whole time.'

'But they had to come and fetch you…I saw them.'

'That's because he was on his way back from getting a scan, and I was with another patient.'

A muscle flicked along the line of his jaw. 'I still think something more could have been done for him—'

'Is there a problem here?' Callum came and stood next to Jade, but he was looking at Stephen's father.

'Yes. I want to know what's happening. I want to know why my son has suddenly collapsed. Someone should have been taking care of him.'

'I'll do my best to answer your questions,' Callum

said. 'We could go along to the relatives' room, where we can sit and talk and have some privacy. Shall we do that? You might be more comfortable in there, and you can maybe get a cup of tea or coffee while you're waiting. We'll need you to sign a consent form for your son's surgery, but I'll talk you through that.'

The man nodded doubtfully. 'All right.'

He glanced at Jade, his brows meeting in a frowning line, and she said quickly, 'I'll keep you informed of what's happening. As soon as there's any news, I'll come and find you.'

Callum lightly touched the man's arm. 'This way.' He turned him in the direction of the relatives' room, and Jade watched them walk away. She was worried about the fact that Callum had found it necessary to intervene. He obviously didn't think she was handling the situation very well, and it didn't look good for her when the consultant had to step in and take over.

There was nothing she could do to remedy the situation, though, so she went back into the treatment room where the surgeon was studying the scans.

'That's a massive aneurysm,' he said. 'If it has already burst, surgery will be touch and go. Judging from his condition, it may already be too late to save him, but I'll do what I can.'

Jade watched as Stephen was wheeled away towards Theatre. It didn't seem right that one minute she had been talking to him and a little later he was fighting for his life. Was there anything more she could have done for him?

'There's a phone call for you,' Katie said. The triage nurse was beckoning her towards Reception, and Jade walked over there, dragging her feet, her mind still with her patient.

Lifting the receiver, she said hello, and heard her brother's voice. She smiled with relief. As she looked across the room, she saw Stephen's father turn to glance at her before Callum waved him into the relatives' room.

'Jade, I'm so glad I managed to catch you,' Ben said. 'I've been trying to get a flight home, but there are storms out at sea, and it looks as though I'm going to have to wait for several more hours yet. I've spoken to Mum, and I tried to talk to Gemma, but she was sleeping and they didn't want to disturb her. How is she? They wouldn't tell me much.'

Jade filled him in as best she could. 'She lost a lot of blood because of the pelvic fracture, and she had to have a transfusion. I'm afraid it'll be a while before she's back on her feet.'

'I've rung the ward on several occasions to try to speak to her, but they wouldn't put me through. I thought perhaps she was trying to avoid me. I wondered if maybe she didn't want to talk to me. Things haven't been going too well between us lately.'

'It's more likely that she was unable to talk—perhaps because the doctor was with her or maybe she was receiving treatment. I'm sure that she would be glad to know that you phoned. It may be that the medical team is worried about her head injury, among other things, and they don't want her to be upset in any way while she's recovering. She hasn't even been able to see the children yet, and I had to keep my visit very short.'

'Perhaps that's it, then. I can't help worrying. I know that she doesn't like me being away so much, but I'm just trying to make a living for Gemma and the children. I want them to have the best.'

'I know you do,' Jade murmured, 'but perhaps they would rather have you home with them. The children have already lost one father, so to speak.'

'That's different. He left them when they were very little. I'd be surprised if they remember very much about him. He doesn't come back and see them, does he? He's never kept in touch.'

'I don't want to tell you how to live your life, Ben, but sometimes the best thing you can do for your family is just to be with them. Do you remember how it was for you after your dad died? You were Rebeccah's age, and I bet what you wanted most was to have him back with you.'

'I will be with them, just as soon as I can get a flight home. I'm hoping that the weather will clear before too long.'

She could hear the restlessness in his tone. 'I hope so, too. Will you give me a ring as soon as you get home?'

'I will. It's good to talk to you, Jade.'

She put the receiver down, mulling over their conversation. Things had to go better for Ben and Gemma—surely they would eventually be able to sort out their marriage problems?

If only she could have a good long talk with Ben. For as far back as she could remember she had been concerned for her brother's welfare. He had been very young when his father had died, just five years old in fact, and he had turned to her for comfort. They were very close…even more so because their mother had succumbed to a nervous breakdown, and it must have seemed as though Jade had been all he'd had.

Their mother's collapse hadn't come as any great surprise to Jade. Her first husband, Jade's father, had left her, and it had taken her a long time to get over their divorce. Then, just as she had been settling into a new life, her second husband had been taken ill and had died, and she had gone to pieces.

Jade gave a shuddery sigh, trying to hold back the memories. She had done what she could to keep the family together, but it had been a hard task for a ten-year-old. She had done her best, though, and her main concern had been to make sure that Ben came through everything all right.

'You're looking very serious,' a voice said close by, and she looked up to see Sam, the paramedic who had brought in the little boy suffering from propranolol poisoning the previous day.

'Hello, Sam.' Still preoccupied with her thoughts, she gave him a brief smile. 'How are things with you?'

'They're much better for seeing you,' he said. 'I was just about to go and get some lunch. Are you due for a break yet? Katie said that you might be free in a few minutes. I thought maybe we could go to the cafeteria together.'

She shook her head. 'Sorry, but I've already made plans for my lunch-break. It's good to see you again, though.'

A shadow crossed his features. 'Is there somebody else? Am I treading on someone's toes?'

'Nothing like that. It's just that I have way too many things to deal with just lately. Don't take it personally.'

She wasn't sure that he was appeased. He sent her a doubtful look, and when he would have hung around Jade said, 'I have to go and check on a patient. Perhaps we'll be able to talk some other time?'

He nodded but didn't seem convinced, and Jade turned away to go in search of the little boy with the chest infection.

'The chest X-ray didn't show up anything too significant,' she told the child's mother, 'but I think we'll go ahead with a course of antibiotics and I'll arrange an appointment for him to see the physiotherapist at a later date. He'll probably benefit from some nebulised medication, so I'll sort that out for you as well.'

She smiled at Taylor and gave him a certificate, which said that he was a brilliant patient. 'You can colour it in, see? And I've a smiley-face sticker for you, too.' She fixed the sticker on his T-shirt, and Taylor left the treatment room holding on to his mother's hand and looking pleased with himself.

Sam was back in A and E when she came back from her lunch-break, and though he tried to make cheerful conversation she was a little subdued in her responses. She had been to see her mother and Gemma, and neither of them was feeling too good. Gemma's head injury was giving some cause for concern, and it worried Jade because she wanted more than anything to be able to give Rebeccah and Connor some positive news.

'Ah, there you are,' Callum said, coming towards her. 'I've been looking for you.'

Sam grimaced and muttered a quick goodbye, before heading towards the exit.

Callum said, 'Your patient's on his way down from

Theatre, and I wanted a word with you about his case—
if it wouldn't be too much trouble in between your
phone calls and other pressing business.' He sent a
glance in Sam's direction, and she guessed he wasn't
too happy that she had been passing the time of day with
him. She didn't see why she should be defensive. Tech-
nically, she had only just finished her lunch-break, and
she didn't have to answer to him about the way she
spent her free time.

'Is there any good news?' she asked. 'The surgeon
wasn't too optimistic.'

Callum grimaced. 'From the sound of it, it was a dev-
astating haemorrhage. Mr Jamieson has managed to
patch him up, but it will all depend on whether he suf-
fers a secondary bleed.'

'He's so young. It must be tragic for his family. Was
he married, do you know?'

'No, he wasn't, but of course his parents are very upset. I've spoken to them. I know he was your patient,
but I thought it best in the circumstances.'

'I wondered about that. Did I do something wrong?'
She looked at him anxiously. She wasn't aware of any
mistakes that she had made, but she was inexperienced
and perhaps she could have handled things differently.
She couldn't think of any other reason why Callum
would have stepped in.

'No, you didn't do anything wrong.' His manner
softened, and he looked at her in a way that gave her
hope. Perhaps she wasn't such a bad doctor after all.

He added, 'Stephen's father was very disturbed by
what happened. He was becoming agitated, and I
thought the situation called for careful handling, so I de-

cided to step in. He was upset because he thought you weren't attending to Stephen's case, but I assured him that you were doing everything possible. I explained that the aneurysm had been dangerously close to bursting when Stephen came in to A and E, and that it was unfortunate that his condition deteriorated before he could receive preventative treatment.'

He sent her a thoughtful glance. 'I told him that you followed all the correct procedures, so you don't have to worry about it. You couldn't have done anything to prevent it from happening.' He gave a brief smile. 'In fact, you did well to pick up on the fact that he was suffering from more than a simple headache.'

Was he actually approving of something she had done? Despite all her attempts to appear independent, she was pleased that he was acknowledging her efforts. It was a relief to have his support.

She said softly, 'You know, I don't blame him for being upset. Even I'm finding it hard to take in. Stephen looked so young and fit. I hope he comes through this all right.'

'So do I.'

He might have said more, but Katie called him away to attend to another patient and Jade didn't see much of him for the rest of the day. She found herself looking for him. It was oddly out of character for her, but it was like a compulsion, a totally fruitless one, because of course he was preoccupied with other things and she was the last person on his mind. She couldn't imagine what was the matter with her.

When her shift came to an end, she went to look in on her mother and Gemma once more before she left for home. Gemma didn't look well, and Jade was worried about her. One way and another, it hadn't been a good day.

The children were cheerful enough, though, when she collected them from Libby's house again and took them back to the cottage.

'Is Daddy really coming back?' Connor wanted to know, when Jade told them that she had spoken to him. 'What did he say?'

'He said that as soon as the weather clears he'll fly home. He's looking forward to seeing you both again.'

Connor began to jump up and down with excitement. 'I can't wait,' he said. Jade glanced at Rebeccah, and saw that she, too, was smiling.

'Why don't you two go and play in the garden while I get dinner ready?' Jade suggested. 'Take the kitten with you. He's been cooped up all day and he could do with some fresh air.'

She wanted to prepare something quick and easy for the evening meal, and she thought that grilled fish steaks with cauliflower cheese would probably suit well enough. As she peeled potatoes, she watched the children from the kitchen window and thought about the day's events.

Stephen had been admitted to Intensive Care, and she could well understand how worried his family was. Did they still blame her for what had happened? Whatever the facts of the matter, she felt that she had in some way failed Stephen. It disturbed her that he was so ill, and she felt helpless. All she could to do now, though, was to go and check on him in the morning.

The doorbell rang as she set the fish under the grill, and she hurried to answer the door, only to find that it was a salesman who wanted to switch her telephone account to a company she never heard of.

'I'm happy with the account I have,' she said, but he was very persistent, and even when her smoke alarm started to sound a warning from the kitchen, he was reluctant to accept her dismissal of him. A minute or two went by as he persisted, but she wasn't too worried. The slightest hint of burnt toast was enough to set the alarm off, but she needed to go and make sure that all was well.

Closing the door on the man, she hurried back to the kitchen and pulled the smoking pan from under the grill, before wafting a newspaper under the alarm. The horrible noise eventually stopped, and when she checked on the fish it still looked all right, so she popped it back under the grill on a lower setting. Within a few minutes, though, the alarm was sounding again, and the children came rushing into the kitchen to see what was happening.

Rebeccah looked worried. 'Is the house on fire?' she asked.

'No, it isn't,' Jade said. 'Fat splatters up onto the metal grill plate behind the element—just there, see— and then it sends out smoke into the kitchen.' She pointed out the protective metal guard. 'It needs cleaning, that's all. As soon as I've cooked dinner, I'll take it out and wash it. You don't need to worry…everything is fine.'

Rebeccah turned on Connor. 'See,' she said. 'I told you there wasn't a fire.'

Connor shrugged. 'So. How was I s'pposed to know? Smoke was coming out of the cooker.'

Jade watched the two of them argue, and warning bells began to sound in her head. Why was Connor looking so defensive? Then she realised that the noise wasn't in her head at all. What she was hearing was actually the sound of a fire engine getting closer, so close, in fact, that it appeared very much as though it was coming from the front of the house.

'You didn't, did you?' She looked at Connor. 'You didn't call the fire brigade, did you?'

Connor didn't answer, but looked down at the floor instead, shuffling from one foot to the other, and there was suddenly a loud knocking at the front door. Jade straightened her shoulders and pulled in a deep breath before going to answer it. Three burly firemen stood outside, hoses at the ready.

'Where's the fire, love? Is it round the back in the kitchen? Let's get everybody out, shall we?'

Jade said weakly, 'I think there's been some mistake.'

'Are you sure?' The lead firemen sniffed the air. 'Something doesn't smell quite right.'

'It's only the grill pan and some burnt-on fat,' Jade explained. 'I was cooking the evening meal and it smoked a bit, but everything is all right, really. I'm sorry if you've had a wasted journey. Connor's only four, and I think he called you by mistake.'

'Did he?' The lead fireman looked behind her. 'Is this the young man who made the call?'

Connor was wide-eyed. He peeped out from behind Jade's skirt and said, 'There was lots of smoke, and the house was nearly on fire and the alarm went off, and it frightened the kitten, and now he's gone up the tree and he won't come down.'

'Really? So you got on the phone and asked for the fire engine, did you?'

Connor nodded, but he was a little less sure of himself this time. These men were big, and they were looking at him oddly.

'Well, you did the right thing if you thought there was a fire,' the man said. 'Perhaps we had better come in and have a look. We might be able to coax the kitten down while we're about it.'

Jade stood back to let them in, then slumped back against the wall. How could this be happening to her? Then she saw that Callum was coming along the path, and her heart started to thump discordantly. He had obviously heard the commotion and come to investigate.

She noticed absently that he must have come home from work and changed into casual clothes, because he was wearing a loose shirt and dark trousers that fitted his long, firmly muscled legs snugly. He looked good, but he also looked worried.

'Is there a fire? Is everybody all right?'

She looked at him helplessly. When he learned the truth he was bound to think that she was a complete idiot. How was she going to explain things?

He frowned. 'What can I do to help?'

'Nothing. It's all right, really.' She shook her head, totally bemused by events, not knowing what to say or how to explain, and for a moment she simply stood there.

He came towards her and put his arm around her shoulders. 'Don't look so worried,' he said. 'We can sort this out. Are the children safe? That's the most important thing.'

'They're fine,' she said, her voice wavering. 'It's all a mistake.' A very big mistake, because now her small cottage was overrun with firemen, and Callum was holding her close as though to protect her from an unseen enemy and his nearness was having a very strange effect on her. She wasn't used to him being so sympathetic and understanding. Even more to the point, she was completely distracted by the way his arms folded around her, as though he would shield her from the outside world. It made the blood rush to her head, and the world began to spin out of control.

'You need to sit down somewhere,' he said. 'Step outside the house where you'll be safe, and I'll go and find the children.'

She didn't know how she was going to tell him. 'There isn't a fire,' she said. 'It was Connor. I think he wanted to see a fire engine…a real fire engine…so he called them out.' She shook her head. 'I don't know what I'm going to do about that boy.'

He stared at her and she wondered what he was thinking. Most likely he was getting ready to give her another dressing down for leaving the children to their own devices. She was totally to blame for everything that had happened, she knew that, and now she waited for the recriminations to start. There was only silence, though, and after a moment or two she looked up at him guardedly.

He said calmly, 'I don't suppose you've thought about the possibility of foster-care?'

Was he serious? She stared at him, open-mouthed. 'I might have known you would make a suggestion like that,' she said stiffly. 'You don't have any understanding of children at all, do you?' She sniffed. 'I expect you were an only child.'

He smiled wryly. 'That was actually meant as a joke,' he said, 'but I can see that you're in no mood for frivolity. Perhaps we should go and find out what your offspring are getting up to now?'

She shook her head. Of course, she had to tell him that they weren't hers, but his grip on her tightened and the words dissolved in her throat as she was enveloped once more in a warm, fuzzy cloud.

He turned her around and led her along the passageway towards the kitchen. His arms stayed firmly around her, as though he thought she might fall, or maybe he was afraid she would try to make a bid for freedom. She wondered vaguely why it was that she was experiencing such a strange reaction to him.

His own responses to the situation were all wrong. She wasn't used to this level of concern, or even such a modicum of understanding, and it didn't make any sense to her. If the truth were known, he had probably only come round here because he thought his property might be about to burn down.

Then again, perhaps she was the one who was out of synch. The whole process of looking after her brother's children was beginning to have a disastrous effect on her, and maybe she was in danger of becoming slightly delirious. Whatever the truth of it, while Callum had his arms around her, she simply couldn't think straight.

CHAPTER FOUR

'THE men are letting the children take a closer look at the fire engine,' Jade said, hurrying back into the kitchen.

Callum nodded. 'I thought they might.' He frowned, glancing over at the hob where pans of steaming vegetables hissed and bubbled. Jade went to take a closer look.

She made some minor adjustments to the gas flame, then turned to face him. 'You know, there was never any real danger of your property burning down.' She felt that she ought to point that out. 'I may not be the best cook in the world, but I do always try my best not to set the place on fire.'

Callum smiled. 'I'm glad to hear it. I must say, I'm rather fond of this cottage and my house next door. I would have been sad to see them go. They've been in the family for years, and they're part of my heritage.'

'Heritage?' She raised finely arched brows. 'That sounds like something you would certainly want to hold onto. Does your family have a special connection with the area around here? I'm fairly new to this part of the Cotswolds. My family home was some twenty miles away.'

He nodded. 'My great-grandparents used to employ people hereabouts. They were mill owners, and apart from their business interests they owned several properties that were passed down through the generations. My grandparents left me these two houses, and my brother and sister inherited others.'

Jade was wide-eyed. 'There were others?' With that kind of history, he must have a vastly wealthy background way out of her league.

'A couple…the Mill House and a country retreat.'

She was awestruck. 'That's an incredible inheritance. You must have a very strong sense of family.' She started to lay the table for dinner and paused momentarily to glance at him. 'Do your parents live locally?'

He nodded. 'They have a place not far from here…a little closer to town, but in a fairly rural area. They've never wanted to stray far from their roots.'

She studied him, her mouth making a crooked line. 'You mentioned a brother and sister, so I guess I was wrong about you being an only child. Are you the oldest?'

He shook his head. 'In fact, I'm the youngest of the three. There's quite a gap between me and my older brother and sister.'

'Ah…that explains a lot.' Jade sent him a knowing look. 'Despite your background, I had the impression that you don't know very much about the way families work…those with young children around, anyway. Do your brother and sister have any children?'

His mouth slanted in a crooked grin. 'Not yet. They both seem to have left it a little late. Up until now my brother has wanted to concentrate on building up his business interests before he started a family…he's following on from my father's work in developing textiles, and his wife is very much a partner in the company. As to my sister, she's been having treatment for endometriosis, but I think she may at last be pregnant. She's wanted a family for a long time.'

Jade smiled. 'She must be thrilled at the prospect, then.' She pulled the pie dish out of the oven and inspected the cauliflower cheese. At least that was coming along without incident.

'Yes, I think she is.' Callum glanced at the dish in her hands. 'That looks good. It smells appetising, too.'

'Do you think so?' Perhaps he was hungry. She had unwittingly taken him from whatever he had been doing at home, and she couldn't help feeling a little glow inside when she thought how quickly he had responded when he had thought they were in danger. He had been concerned for their safety, and he had shown that he was prepared to take care of them all. She hadn't expected that, and it warmed her through and through.

She said, 'I seem to have made rather a lot of food, probably much more than we can manage. Have you already eaten, or would you like to stay for dinner?' The offer was out before she had time to consider, but now she stopped to take stock. What was she doing? It was like inviting the enemy into her camp. He was her boss, for heaven's sake, He could be hauling her over the coals in the morning for making a hash of a simple procedure at work.

'Thank you, I'd like that…if you're sure it would be no trouble?'

'It's no trouble at all.' She made an effort to cover up

her doubts. The deed was done, and there was no going back on it now. Jade pulled in a deep breath.

The children ran in from outside, and she put the dish back into the oven and listened to their excited clamour.

'I went up on the ladder,' Connor exclaimed. 'It was well good.' His eyes were sparkling. 'And the fireman let me hold the hose…but he wouldn't let me switch the water on.' He frowned at that, but then reverted to joyfully hopping about the kitchen, almost bowling into Callum. Callum put out an arm to steady him.

'I went up the ladder as well, and the fireman showed me the driver's cab,' Rebeccah said, her face lighting up as she recounted the experience. 'He let me hold onto the steering-wheel.'

'It sounds as though you both had a lot of fun.' Jade gave them a light hug. 'You should go and wash your hands for dinner while I go and talk to the firemen. I expect they'll want to be on their way.' She glanced at Callum. 'Would it be all right if I leave the children with you for a moment?'

Callum nodded, but looked doubtful at the prospect. He watched the children warily as they danced around the kitchen, and she wondered if he thought they were some kind of alien species.

Jade watched the firemen preparing to leave. She was deeply apologetic over the false callout, and luckily there were no repercussions. Thankfully the firemen took it all in good part, and she vowed to keep Connor well away from the phone from then on.

Going back into the kitchen, she saw that Connor was still telling Callum all about the fire engine and

Rebeccah was chipping in with her two pennyworth every now and again. The children were full of it, even after she had served up the meal.

'I'm going to tell Mummy all about it,' Connor said, tucking into his dinner and waving his fork in the air. 'I'm going to paint a picture of the fire engine and give it to her.' He looked at Jade for confirmation, and she nodded acknowledgement. He had been so excited that he had almost finished his meal without a single complaint.

Callum looked puzzled. 'I think your mummy already knows,' he said gently. 'She let the firemen into the house, remember?' He glanced at Jade, and she opened her mouth to speak, wondering where to begin, but Rebeccah cut in.

'No, she didn't. She can't. Mummy's in hospital.' She looked at him pityingly. 'Didn't you know?'

He shook his head, looking completely fazed for a moment, and then he turned to Jade and said with a frown, 'So you're not their mother?'

'No.' She hesitated, standing up to remove the dinner plates from the table and replace them with the dessert. 'Rebeccah and Connor are my half-brother's children.'

He frowned. 'Why didn't you tell me?'

Jade said quickly, 'I meant to tell you. There just never seemed to be an opportunity, and then I kept forgetting that you didn't know.'

'And their mother is in hospital?'

'Yes, that's right…along with my mother.' She saw that the children were engrossed in spooning fruit crumble and custard into their mouths and weren't paying very much attention to what she was saying. Then they started a noisy argument over who had the larger portion. 'They were both injured when a car ran into them, so I'm taking care of the children.'

'That makes a few things suddenly seem a whole lot clearer.' He stared at her, sending her a dark, probing glance. 'I'm still concerned, though, that you felt you had to cope on your own. Couldn't you have told me? Wouldn't it have been simpler to ask for help, in the circumstances?'

Jade could see that he wasn't taking her omission very well. She shook her head. 'No, not really. What could you have done, anyway? Besides, I'm used to managing on my own. Over the years I've found that I need to be able to sort out my own problems.' She made a wry grimace. 'Anyway, who would want to help out with two squabbling kids?'

He glanced at the children, and he was thoughtful as he turned his attention to the dessert, though there was still a frown in his eyes. It bothered Jade that she had in some way left him disappointed in her, but she doubted that he would ever understand her point of view.

She guessed that he had a much more straightforward outlook. When had he ever had to deal with the unexpected? His way of life was probably secure and protected, bowling along without undue incident. He was used to being in command, in control of his own destiny, and he wouldn't be able to easily accept that some people had to be constantly on their guard against adversity.

She, on the other hand, had grown used to life knocking her back, and she had learned to roll with the punches. Most of all, she had learned never to put her trust in anyone because, when all was said and done, you could never depend on them being around when it mattered most.

Rebeccah broke the brief silence. 'Can we go and see Mummy in hospital?'

'I hope so,' Jade said quietly. 'I'll talk to the doctors about it tomorrow and try to arrange something. Perhaps they'll let you see her, even if it's for just a little while.'

'I want to take her a picture and some flowers,' Connor put in.

Jade nodded. 'Yes, we'll do that.'

'And we'll give Nanna some flowers as well,' Rebeccah put in. 'She'll like that.'

'I'm sure she will.'

Callum asked, 'How are they doing? Are they making progress?'

'Slowly, yes. These are early days yet, but my mother seems to be improving. She has a shoulder fracture, but it appears to be healing without any undue problems. My sister-in-law needs a little more care and attention.' She glanced at the children, not wanting to upset them in any way, and she was relieved that they had both reverted to seeing who had more custard left. 'They've managed to stabilise her pelvis fracture, but she had a head injury, too, and that's giving a little cause for concern. They've given her medication to minimise the after-effects, but it tends to make her drowsy.'

'I'm sorry. This must be difficult for you.'

'It's been something of a challenge, I'll say that much.' She glanced at the children. Rebeccah had finished her meal and was getting restless, and now Connor was making a noise like the siren of a fire engine.

'Can I wear my new T-shirt for the trip tomorrow?' Rebeccah looked eagerly at Jade. 'My teacher says we can take some money to spend in the shop, and I want to get some crystals for Mummy. She says we can only take a little bit, though.' She gave her brother a superior look. 'Connor thinks he can take pounds and pounds.'

Connor stopped shrieking and stuck his tongue out at his sister, while Callum looked on, bemused.

Jade sucked in a quick breath. 'The trip—with everything that's happened, I'd almost forgotten about that. I'll have to get your things ready.' Jade nodded towards Rebeccah. 'Yes, sweetheart, I'll sort your T-shirt out.'

Callum glanced from one to the other and said quietly, 'The meal was delicious. Thank you for that, Jade.' He pushed back his chair. 'I think I should be getting back home. There are some things I need to do, and I can see that you have your hands full here.'

She couldn't read his brooding expression, but she guessed that he was somewhat subdued, and she wondered if that was because she hadn't been straight with him from the first. Still, it was too late to remedy the situation now.

She showed him out, then went back to the children, who by now were chasing each other around the kitchen table. Calming them down, she sent them out to play.

Thinking about it, Callum's preoccupation was much more likely to have resulted from him having been included in the mayhem that passed for an evening meal in her household. Dinner with his family was probably a much more civilised affair. He wasn't used to children, and it only went to show what a gaping chasm there was between their separate lifestyles.

She wondered if the children would ever adjust to being away from home and settle down, but things didn't get any better as time went on. There was just as much chaos to contend with in the household next morning, and by the time she had waved the children off into school she was stressed out. She only just made it in to work on time by the skin of her teeth.

Callum glanced at the clock as she hurried into A and E and frowned. 'More problems?' he asked.

'We had a few setbacks,' she said, still trying to catch her breath after the rush, 'but I'll get the hang of things before too long, I hope.'

'Don't you think you've taken on more than you can handle? Those children aren't necessarily your concern. There are other alternatives you could consider.'

She frowned at that. How could he be so cool and dismissive about her family obligations? 'You may not agree, but I don't see that I have any choice. They are my flesh and blood after all. I certainly wouldn't let them go to strangers.' She stared at him. 'Perhaps you don't have the same feelings of loyalty towards your family?'

'It's never actually been put to the test,' he admitted. 'But the circumstances are different in your case. You've taken on a difficult job, here in A and E, and you're relatively inexperienced in emergency work. It isn't going to help you to do your job properly if your mind is constantly elsewhere.'

'That's as may be,' she shot back, 'but I wouldn't

dream of sending them away. As it is, they're upset enough about what's happened. Their world has been turned upside down. They've suddenly lost the support of their mother and grandmother, their stepfather is working away, and I'm surely not going to add to their problems by having them lose me as well.' She glared at him, her green eyes flint sharp.

He didn't pursue the matter any further, simply returning her stare with a cool scrutiny of his own, and she recalled that she was at work and that time was at a premium. She tried to gather her thoughts. A fleeting moment of unease had her checking her bag to make sure that she had put her car keys in there.

'So,' he said, his tone tinged with irony, 'what went wrong this morning—did they flood the house, or somehow manage to lose the kitten?'

Glancing at him distractedly, she echoed, 'Kitten?'

She found the keys and started to pull on her white jacket in preparation for the day ahead. Shrugging into it, she began to hunt through her pockets for her stethoscope.

'The animal that you've adopted,' he said. 'The strange furry thing with the big eyes.'

She blinked. 'Oh, you mean Kizzy—no, the kitten's fine. His owner came round and said that the mother cat had been depositing her kittens in gardens where she thought the family would be suitable to look after them. She thought—the owner, I mean—that Rebeccah and Connor would be good for him and she said they could keep him if they wanted.'

She found the stethoscope, and then started a search for her bleeper. 'Actually, it was all my fault that we were late today—I mislaid Connor's holdall. Anyway, we sorted everything out in the end. They're away on a trip to a National Trust house and gardens. You'd think they were going to the moon, with all the preparations involved.'

'I can imagine it,' he said dryly. 'I wouldn't care to be their teacher. One child could be difficult, two a handful, and a whole class would have me reaching for the aspirin. Your two on their own are like a menagerie.'

She started on another search, and he watched her, his brows drawing together in a dark line. 'What have you lost this time?'

'My pen—no, here it is.' She slotted it into her jacket pocket. 'I don't think they're normally as excitable as they have been the last few days, but with their mother being in hospital, they're a bit confused and out of synch and they need an outlet for all those bewildering emotions.'

'You're probably right—it seems to me, though, that this is all adding up to a huge strain on you. I hope you're going to be able to get your head around work.' He looked at her as though he had grave doubts about that. 'We've just had notification of a lorry crashing down an embankment and into a motorway services restaurant. There were a lot of casualties and they're being sent to various hospitals around and about. Some of them are on their way here. They're expected to arrive within the next fifteen minutes or so, and it means that we're going to have our hands full for the next few hours.'

She sucked in a quick breath. 'That sounds nasty. I'll go and check up on supplies.'

The morning passed in a desperate rush. Casualties

were still being brought in a couple of hours later, as the emergency services managed to work their way through twisted metal and rubble and clear a way to the people who were injured.

Sam brought in a man who was suffering from a chest injury. 'He was trapped under some fallen masonry,' the paramedic told Jade. 'He seems to have been lucky. It could have been much worse, given that it's taken so long to free him, but he doesn't appear to have any other major injuries.'

'Thanks, Sam.'

She turned to her patient, who was struggling to get his breath. 'I'm going to make a quick examination of you, Andy,' she said. 'Does it hurt you to breathe?'

Andy nodded, and a nurse came to help him with the oxygen mask. 'It looks as though you've broken several of your ribs,' Jade murmured after a while, 'but I think we'll get an X-ray so that we can be sure exactly what's happened.' She listened to his heart, and was disturbed to find that it was racing. He was very pale and his skin was cold to the touch, and she was worried that he might be going into shock and was perhaps bleeding internally. 'Is there someone we can contact for you? Your wife, perhaps?'

He started to speak, but then his breathing worsened, and Jade could see that he was struggling with the effort. She told Helen, 'We need to take some blood to send for cross-matching, and I'll probably need to put in a chest drain.'

She worked swiftly and saw that Sam was still hanging around. 'I'm waiting for my partner,' he said. 'He's bringing in a woman with leg injuries.'

'It was a horrendous accident, wasn't it?' she murmured.

Sam nodded. 'Not the sort of thing you want to see every day.' On a lighter note he added, 'The only good outcome is that I get to see more of you.'

Jade made a weak smile. 'I wouldn't say these were the ideal circumstances for a meeting.' She glanced at him fleetingly. 'Look, I have to get back to work—I need to put in a chest tube.'

Sam grimaced, but left her to get on with it, and she explained to Andy what she was about to do. 'This will help to relieve the pressure on your lungs, and your breathing should improve,' she told him. She was a little worried about putting in the tube—if she inserted it too far, or in the wrong place, her patient would be in trouble, but she didn't tell Andy that.

Luckily, Callum came along to watch over what she was doing. 'What's happening here?' he asked.

'There's bleeding into the chest cavity—it's beginning to affect his breathing, and I'm afraid that he might slip into shock.'

Callum studied the patient. 'There's definitely a haemothorax. I'll talk you through the procedure,' he said.

Relieved that she wasn't on her own, she prepared to make the incision, but her patient was suddenly totally unresponsive and she was worried that things were taking a downward turn. Helen said, 'I'll try to contact his wife—we managed to find a phone number for her.'

Jade nodded, but continued with the procedure. She identified the fifth intercostal space and began to infiltrate the area with local anaesthetic.

'Make your incision in the line of the ribs,' Callum said. 'That's right—infiltrate more anaesthetic down to the top of the sixth rib. Now use the artery forceps to spread the tissues down to the pleural space and puncture the pleura. That's good. OK, now put the tip of your finger into the pleural cavity and make sure that you have a clear passage to insert the chest drain.'

She followed his instructions and inserted the chest drain, connecting it to an underwater seal, and then she sutured the drain securely in place.

Helen came back just then. 'Callum, we need you— Dr Franklin's patient has gone into cardiac arrest.'

'Are you all right to finish off here?' Callum asked, looking at Jade, and she nodded.

He walked away briskly, and she covered the incision she had made with a dressing and adhesive tape. Then she checked to make sure that the underwater seal was swinging in the tube with the phases of respiration. At last her patient's condition was beginning to improve, and he mumbled something incoherent, something that she didn't quite catch.

'You're going to be all right, Andy,' she reassured him. 'I'm going to take an X-ray to make sure everything is in place as it should be.'

He said something else that she couldn't quite make out, and she said, 'Try not to worry. Your wife is on her way here. The nurse told me she'll be with you in a little while.'

The news didn't have quite the effect that Jade expected. She saw alarm flare in his eyes, and she frowned, but when she gently questioned him, he didn't reply. He appeared to be agitated, and she checked to see that all was well and that he was not in pain. Then a noise behind her alerted her to the fact that they were not alone.

'How is he?' a woman said. 'The nurse told me what happened. I don't understand…'

'Are you Mrs Johnson?'

'I'm his wife, yes. They told me that he had broken some ribs.' She looked beyond Jade to the bed where Andy was lying, conscious but not speaking, his eyes wide and clearly troubled. 'I heard about the lorry going into the service station—it was on the local news. I couldn't believe it—I don't know what he was doing there.'

Jade glanced at her patient. 'Perhaps I should leave you two to talk?'

Andy gave a faint nod, but he was looking apprehensive, and she wondered what was amiss.

She asked Helen to monitor his condition while she went to see to her other patients. There were a lot of people in A and E. They were crowded out with victims of the accident, and relatives were waiting, anxious to hear news. Jade concentrated on working her way through her list of patients, dealing with them as quickly and efficiently as she could.

A short time later she went to check on Andy's condition, but his wife was coming out of the treatment room just as Jade arrived there. She was in tears, and Jade put an arm around her shoulders and led her away.

'What's wrong?' Jade asked. 'Is there anything I can do to help?'

The woman shook her head. 'I can't take it in. I can't believe this is happening.'

'Perhaps you need to go and sit down for a while.'

'He said he went to the service station so that he could fill up the car with petrol and then he went to think things through over breakfast,' the woman said, crying quietly. 'He shouldn't have been there. I couldn't understand what he was doing there, but he just told me he was going to leave the children and me. He was going to leave his job and take up a new offer in another town.' She looked at Jade in despair. 'I didn't know any of this. He hadn't said a word to me about it before today.'

'I'm so sorry.'

The woman wiped a hand over her tear-streaked face. 'How could he do that? How could he plan on going without saying anything at all...without any warning?' She shook her head. 'What can I say to the children? How am I supposed to tell them that their father doesn't want to be with them anymore? They're only six and seven years old.'

'You must be feeling dreadful,' Jade said. 'Is there anyone close to you that you could talk to? Your mother, a sister, perhaps...or a friend?'

'I don't know...maybe my sister... I can't take any of this in.'

'This must have come as a terrible shock to you. Let me take you to the relatives' room. You can have some privacy in there.'

She led the woman away, and talked to her quietly for a few minutes. It was a horrible situation, and she didn't know what she could do to comfort the woman. She said, 'I'm going to get a nurse to come and stay with you, and perhaps arrange for your sister to come over to be with you. I can see that you're very upset. You've had a nasty jolt, and it might help if I get you a cup of tea and then you can sit and talk for a while.'

Jade was conscious that she had to go and attend to her other patients, but she was loath to leave this poor woman alone with her distress. It was bad enough for her to find that her husband was injured, but even worse to discover that he was planning on leaving his family without saying a word.

Except that it wasn't unheard of, was it? Hadn't a similar thing happened within her family? She knew only too well what it was like to be abandoned, tossed aside as though you were no longer wanted. Her father hadn't left as abruptly as Andy, but all the same he had gone away and he had never come back.

The memories swept over her in a tidal wave and the shock of remembrance hit her with full force so that the blow was like a physical pain.

How were those poor children going to feel when they looked for their father and he wasn't there for them? The image flooded her with sadness. There was nothing she could do to make the situation any better for them, though, and that made her feel doubly helpless.

'I'll be back in a second or two,' she told the woman, and tried to push the fragments of memory aside as she went to find a nurse who could take over from her. She quickly explained the situation to Katie, and only when she was sure that the woman was being looked after did she walk slowly back to A and E. She needed time to think, to get her head around this untimely reminder of her own bleak past.

'Jade—wait a moment.'

She looked up, and saw that Callum was coming towards her. She stared at him blankly, her thoughts all over the place, her mind still far away. 'I was going to check on my patients,' she mumbled.

'I know, but you look upset. You should take a moment to calm down.'

She hesitated, aware of a hollow space inside her, as though all feeling had washed out of her. Seeing her falter, he put an arm around her shoulders and even in her dazed state she was conscious of his quiet concern. He led her to the side of the room, to a quiet recess where they could be relatively safe from prying eyes. 'Tell me what's wrong?'

'It's nothing,' she said awkwardly. 'I mean, I haven't lost a patient or anything. It isn't to do with work, really.' Having his arm around her was some consolation. It made her feel warm and comforted.

'But something is bothering you. Do you want to tell me about it?'

'There's nothing you can do. I'll be fine.' She didn't want him to see her misery, and she looked away, staring at nothing, until he reached out and laid his cupped hand under her chin and tilted her face upwards so that she had to look into his eyes. 'What is it?' he murmured. 'What's happened?'

She made a little shuddery sigh. 'It seems so silly… I don't know why I'm upset. It was all such a long time ago.' She hesitated, trying to compose herself. Callum was waiting patiently for an answer and here she was, just babbling.

She tried turning away once more, but he wasn't going to let her go until she told him what was on her mind. Gently, he brought her around to face him once more. 'Out with it,' he said.

She moistened her lips with the tip of her tongue. 'I've been talking to the wife of one of my patients—the man with the haemothorax. Apparently he was leaving his wife and children when the accident happened. He didn't have the courage to tell them that he was going, but just quietly left them behind. Can you imagine how those children would have felt? They would have looked for him, and waited, and their hopes would all have been dashed.'

He said softly, 'You can't take everyone's problems on board, you know. It's enough that you mend their broken bodies, without taking on their emotional pain as well.'

'I do know that… But it suddenly brought it all back to me… It made me remember how I felt when my own father left.'

He frowned. 'It must have been hard for you to cope with something like that.'

She struggled to stop her voice from shaking. 'I don't know why it upset me so much just now—after all, it was a long time ago. Perhaps it's because of Rebeccah and Connor. I know how disturbed they've been because their mother isn't there for them. It doesn't show on the surface, but it's there in the way they behave. They're excitable, volatile and thoroughly unsettled, and I know it's more difficult for them because their real father left them, too. It was some time ago, but they have flashes of memory from time to time and I try to help them through it as best I can.'

'It sounds as though you know exactly what they're going through.'

She nodded. 'I think I do, in a way. My parents divorced when I was just a little girl, and I didn't really know what was happening, but I knew that it was bad. I desperately wanted them to stay together, but things fell apart and there came a time when my father left and didn't come back. I didn't understand what was going on and I think I was worried that my mother might leave me, too.'

'How old where you, then?'

'I think I was about four years old when they separated. I must have been five when I last saw him. I suppose I felt that I was somehow to blame for everything that happened.'

He put his arms around her, drawing her close, and it felt good, having him hold her that way. She felt warm and sheltered, as though she had found a safe haven from the storm. 'You must know that you weren't to blame,' he murmured, comforting the small child inside her. 'Haven't you found out why they split up?'

She pulled in a shaky breath. 'Yes. Of course, you're right… I know now that I wasn't to blame. My mother wanted to explain, to help me to understand, and she's talked about it over the years. From what I gather, the marriage was hastily arranged…my mother was already pregnant with me, and I suppose my father thought that he'd been somehow tricked into marriage. He wasn't ready for a family.'

'He's probably a lot older and wiser now, and he might see things in a different light. Have you tried to get in touch with him?'

'No. I would never do that. I don't want to know him.' The words came out with perhaps more vehemence than she'd intended, and she added on a calmer note, 'I really don't want anything to do with him.'

She heard the sound of a trolley being wheeled nearby, and she glanced around, suddenly aware that life was still going on all around her. She had been so taken up with her thoughts and so warmed by Callum's caring, compassionate manner that everything else had gone from her mind.

She looked at him warily. It was crazy, but she wanted to stay here, wrapped in his embrace, even though it probably meant nothing to him. He was simply trying to comfort her. She said slowly, 'I should get back to work.'

He straightened. 'Me, too.' He seemed to hesitate, but then he let her go, and for a moment she felt chilled through and through, as though she had been abandoned all over again.

'Are you going to be all right?' He was looking at her as though he had serious doubts about that, and she wondered if the professional side of him was trying to gauge whether she could safely be left to return to her work.

She nodded. 'I'll be fine.' It was a gross distortion of the truth. Being in his arms had left her feeling even more troubled than before. It made her long for something that was beyond her reach, some indefinable, nebulous prize that tantalised and tormented her.

She started to walk back with him to the main area of A and E, and as she went by the supplies room she saw that Sam was standing just a short distance away.

He was frowning, and she wondered how long he had been there, watching them.

Helen came hurrying towards them. 'Jade, your patient is going into shock. The man with the haemothorax—he's having difficulty with his breathing again.'

Jade hurried to find out what was going on. 'Perhaps the blood loss was greater than we thought,' she said worriedly. 'I need to check the drainage bottle.'

Callum was already checking it. 'Did you leave it like this?' he asked her.

She glanced in his direction and frowned. The tube was bent in the middle, and the bottle was placed at a higher level than would allow for proper drainage. 'I don't understand.' She shook her head.

'It should have been placed lower than the level of the patient. Not only that, but the tube is kinked because of the way it was positioned.'

'I'm sure I left it as it should be. Everything was working just fine when I left him.'

'Well, it isn't working properly now.' He lowered the bottle and checked to see that the patient's respiration was improving. 'Helen, I want you to stay with him and make regular observations. I'm not happy with the way things are going. It looks as though he's losing far more blood than we first imagined.'

'Could there have been a rupture of an internal artery?' Jade asked.

His expression was grim. 'It looks that way. We need to get him to Theatre, fast.' He did what he could to help lessen the patient's respiratory distress.

'I'll go and call for a cardiothoracic surgeon,' Jade said worriedly.

By now, Andy had recovered enough to be able to gasp out a few words. 'What's happening to me?'

She looked at him and hesitated. Then she said, 'We think that you're bleeding internally.' She tried to forget about the abominable way that he was treating his wife and children, and spoke to him as she would to any patient. 'It could be that your broken ribs have ruptured an artery, and we need to fix that. We're going to send you up to Theatre, so that the surgeon can stop the bleeding and perhaps remove any rough edges from the broken ribs.'

She would have said more, but Callum stepped in and said, 'You should go and attend to your other patients. I'll take over here.'

She sent him a shocked glance. Was he blaming her for what happened? She was sure that she had left the drainage bottle in the right position. She frowned.

She said in a low voice, 'But he's my patient.'

He moved away from the bedside and led her to the door. 'I think it would be for the best if you leave him to me. You had a bad start to the day, coming in at a rush and with your mind all over the place, and now you're emotionally wiped out. We're all under pressure here. We have to be able to rely on one another.'

'I can still do my job…'

'It isn't up for discussion. Go and take a break for half an hour.'

He was leaving her no choice but to go, and the whole episode had left her feeling drained. Just a few moments ago he had been holding her, attempting to soothe her troubles away, and now it was as if that care and tender concern meant nothing at all. In his eyes she had failed her patient, and he wasn't listening to her denials of any wrongdoing. It hurt tremendously that Callum didn't believe in her.

CHAPTER FIVE

'SEE, Mummy? We brought you some flowers. I picked them from out of the garden, especially for you.' Rebeccah laid the flowers carefully in her mother's arms.

'Oh, they're so beautiful,' Gemma said. 'Thank you, angel. Come and give me a kiss.' Rebeccah happily obliged, standing on tiptoe at the side of the hospital bed and leaning over to give her mother a hug.

'I've brought you some as well,' Connor piped up, eager to get in on the act.

'I know you have…and they're lovely, too. I want a big kiss from you, sweetheart.'

Gemma cuddled her children, and they told her all about the kitten, and the fire engine, and how Jade had promised to take them to the park later in the week.

'It sounds as though you're having a lovely time,' she said. 'I hope you're being good for your Auntie Jade.'

'We are,' Connor said, looking as though butter wouldn't melt in his mouth. 'She said if we were good we could have some money for the school trip, and so we were good.'

Gemma smiled. 'I wondered how you and Rebeccah managed to buy me those lovely crystals,' she murmured. 'I shall treasure them. Thank you very much.'

After a while, the children went to play at the side of the room with toys that they had brought with them, and Gemma looked at Jade and said, 'Thank you so much for looking after them, and for bringing them to see me. It's such a relief to know that they're safe. I wanted to come home, but the doctors won't hear of it just yet. They want to make sure that the healing is well under way before they let me out, and they say that I'll need some physiotherapy.'

'You're looking much better than you did when I saw you last,' Jade murmured. 'The children have been asking about you every day.'

'Have they? I miss them so much.' She lowered her voice. 'I haven't heard anything from Ben yet. There was just a quick phone call the other day, but he said he was still waiting for a flight out.'

'There are storms out at sea, and they're keeping the helicopters grounded,' Jade said. 'I'm sure he'll be here as soon as he can.'

'Maybe, but I can't help wondering if he's holding back. He never seems entirely at ease when he's at home. The truth is, I don't think he really knows how to relate to Rebeccah and Connor. They're not his children, and perhaps that's the problem…he probably wishes that he had never married me. I don't suppose he knew what he was taking on, and now he's finding that he can't cope with a ready-made family.'

Jade shook her head. 'I think you're wrong about

that. He loves you. I know he's my brother, and that I'm bound to be loyal to him, but he's always spoken very fondly about you and the children.'

'Talk is easy—it doesn't cost anything, does it? It doesn't make up for the fact that he isn't here, living with us day by day. He comes home every now and again, but he only stays around for a few weeks. We just start getting used to having him around and then he's off to the rigs again.' There was an edge of bitterness in Gemma's voice. She glanced at the children, perhaps feeling guilty about her outburst, and then said on a different note, 'I shouldn't be laying all this on you. I'm out of sorts, being stuck in here, that's the problem.'

'I'm here to help in any way I can,' Jade murmured. 'Do you want to talk to me about it? I'm not going to take sides. I just want both of you to be happy.'

'No. It's best left alone. I'll talk to Ben when he gets here.' She lifted her chin, as though she was strengthening her resolve to put the matter aside. 'Have you been to see your mother? How is she getting on?'

Jade was worried about Gemma's marriage problems, but she didn't want to push the issue and risk upsetting her sister-in-law. Accepting the change of subject, she said quietly, 'She's getting better slowly. I think they would have let her come home if it was just the shoulder that was troubling her, but they want to make sure that there are no more abdominal problems. She sends her love.'

Gemma smiled. 'Louise is a lovely person, and she's always so good with the children. I really miss her.'

'I could ask the nurses on her ward if she can have a wheelchair and come down to see you from time to

time, if you would like that. I know that she would like
to see you.'

Gemma nodded. 'Yes, I'd love to see her.' She
frowned, and then said, 'I haven't asked you about your
new job, have I? You've just started a stint in A and E,
haven't you? How is it working out?'

'It's all right, I suppose. There's a lot of adjusting to
do, because everything seems so immediate in A and E.
It can be frenetic, and I'm always afraid of making a
mistake.'

She wasn't going to tell Gemma about the subarachnoid patient who had given her such a shock by collaps-
ing, or about the man with the haemothorax. He had
gone up to Theatre and now he, at least, was making a
good recovery. She doubted that Callum would believe
that any thanks were due to her for that, though, and it
still hurt that he mistrusted her over the incident with
the drainage tube.

How could her relationship with him have changed
so swiftly? Not so long before that he had comforted
her when she had been upset over her father's callous
departure, and he had held her close so that for a while
she had felt safe and secure in his arms. The warm feelings had soon disappeared, like brittle leaves blown
away by an autumn gale, and maybe that was a kind of
warning to her. Callum was her boss. He would always
put work first, and she should guard against thinking
that he might have any other feelings for her.

'It must be difficult. It's certainly not something that
I could do.' Gemma looked at her searchingly. 'Are you
getting along all right with your boss? You said he was

an older man, didn't you? I think you said you quite liked him after you met him at the interview.'

Jade grimaced. A lot of water had gone under the bridge since then, and as to getting along with Callum, that was all overturned. After the calamity with the chest drain yesterday, he had been totally impassive. She didn't know what to think.

'Things didn't turn out quite the way I expected. The consultant was taken ill—he's been in the renal unit for some time, but at least he's on the mend now. It will be a long while before he comes back to work, though.' She hesitated. 'Actually, my new boss lives next door to me. He owns both properties.'

'Good heavens. It's a small world, isn't it?'

'It's not small,' Connor put in, coming over to the bedside. 'He's got a big, big house.' Jade winced. She hadn't thought that he'd been listening to their conversation. 'You should see his kitchen—it's 'normous,' Connor went on. 'He's got a big bar thing in the middle of the room, and you can sit round it, and some of it's got cupboards underneath, but he's still got a table and chairs in his kitchen.' His eyes were wide with the wonder of it.

'I peeped into his living room,' Rebeccah said earnestly. 'It's got glass doors, and he says he opens them up in the summer and goes out into the garden.'

'And there's a pond in the garden—with real fish,' Connor said, his eyes growing larger by the minute. 'I'm going to ask him if I can look at it properly.'

'I expect he'll be too busy to be wanting to show us around,' Jade said, nipping that idea in the bud. Probably the last thing Callum would want was to have

Rebeccah and Connor going round to his house and disturbing his peace.

She glanced at Gemma. 'I ought to be getting these two home,' she said. It had been easier to collect them from Libby's house and bring them straight to the hospital, rather than to go home and make a special journey, but now it was getting late. She still had the evening meal to prepare and chores to tackle. Besides, Gemma was beginning to look tired. 'I'll bring them to see you again soon.'

'Thanks, Jade. I really appreciate what you're doing.'

'You take care, and get yourself well again. And try not to worry. I'm sure Ben will be home any day now. He told me he wanted to be with you as soon as was humanly possible.'

Jade was thoughtful on the journey back home. It worried her that her brother's marriage didn't appear to be working out. She could understand Gemma's point of view—most of the time Ben wasn't there for her, and she was lonely, feeling that she had to cope alone. She felt as though she was a failure, and that perhaps she could never be happy in a relationship.

It wasn't surprising that she felt that way. Things hadn't worked out with her first husband. He had gone off the rails, and perhaps they had both been too young to make a go of it. Now it looked as though her marriage to Ben was on rocky ground as well.

Jade pulled in a shaky breath. Was this the way of things? All around her she could see people making a mess of their relationships, and it made her even more wary of commitment.

At work next day she was aware that Callum was still

watching her every move, and it made her uncomfortable to feel that she wasn't trusted. What choice did she have, though, but to accept that she must be supervised? The incident with the drainage tube was still clearly at the forefront of his mind, and as the acting consultant it was his responsibility to make sure that all was well. She could hardly blame him for his vigilance.

All she could do was to try to make the best of things and disregard his constant presence, and when an infant was brought in looking dreadfully ill, she pushed all her uncertainties to one side and hurried to assess her condition.

'You said that you've been having problems with feeding her before this collapse?' she queried, glancing at the child's mother.

The woman nodded. There were two other children with her, and she looked pale and tired. 'She hasn't been able to keep much down. She doesn't seem herself at all.' She broke off as her small son tried to climb up on to her lap alongside the infant. 'Not just now, Matthew. I need to talk to the doctor. Go and play with the toys in the corner for a minute.'

Turning back to Jade, she went on, 'She's tired, and not interested in anything, and a lot of the time she doesn't even have the energy to play. That isn't like Alice, she's usually such a lively child. I hate to see her like this.'

Matthew wasn't accepting what his mother told him. He looked to be about four years old, and he complained loudly, 'I want to go on your knee. Don't want to play with the toys.'

'You can't come on my knee while I'm holding Alice,' his mother said. 'Just go and play for a little while, while I talk to the doctor.' She glanced at Jade. 'She looks so ill. I'm really worried about her.' The boy started to wail, objecting to being thwarted.

'She certainly looks poorly,' Jade acknowledged softly, quickly examining the infant. She showed the little girl her smiley-face spatula and managed to persuade her to open her mouth and let her look down her throat. 'She's feverish and not very responsive, and it looks as though she's having some problems with her breathing. It may be that she has an infection of some sort.'

By now, Matthew was hitting his older brother with a toy truck, and the other boy retaliated by giving him a swift kick.

'Jacob, Matthew—stop that.' Mrs Sawyer looked apologetically at Jade. 'I'm still waiting for my husband to come from work and take them off my hands. When I saw the state Alice was in, I just left everything and came straight here.' She pulled in a deep breath. 'She did have a bit of a cough a while back. I took her to my GP, and she had some medicine, but I don't think the cough has cleared up properly.'

Alice was lying limply in her mother's arms, and Jade was worried that this was more than a simple chest infection. Alice's condition was degenerating visibly, her level of consciousness dimming, and Jade was concerned that she might be suffering from septicaemia.

Jade told the mother quietly, 'Sometimes, when an infection takes hold, toxins form in the blood, and they can cause the child to go downhill quite rapidly. I've taken a throat swab, and I'm going to take some blood for testing, so that we can find out what's causing the problem. We'll do an X-ray of her chest as well.'

'What do you think is wrong with her? Do you have any idea?'

'I think it could be pneumonia, but we'll have to wait for the results of the tests in order to confirm that. In the meantime, she's dehydrated, so I'm going to put her on intravenous fluids, and we'll give her oxygen to help with her breathing. We'll have to admit her to the hospital, so that we can monitor her condition.'

The two boys were still fighting, and just as Jade was about to call for them to quieten down, Callum walked into the treatment room. 'What's going on in here?' he demanded.

Jade stared at him, shocked by his sudden entrance.

He said tersely, 'I can hear the racket you're making in the room next door.' He looked at the boys and said firmly, 'If you two go on fighting and making all this noise and disturbing other patients, I shall send you out of here and you'll wait somewhere else where no one will be able to hear you. It's your choice. What will it be? Shall I send for a nurse to take you away from here, or are you going to stay here and settle down?'

The two boys gawped at him. He had their full attention, and neither of them moved a muscle.

'Well?' Callum asked.

'Stay here,' the boys muttered.

Their mother looked uncomfortable, crestfallen because her boys were in trouble on top of everything else that she was going through, but it was Jade who was on the receiving end of Callum's cool glance. Was he blaming her for not keeping things under control? Her cheeks flushed with warm colour. Her patient was her priority, and sorting out quarrels came a poor second to that. Even so, Callum was obviously not impressed by her management of the situation.

She said, 'We've nearly finished in here anyway. I'm going to arrange for Alice to be moved to a side room while we try to find a bed for her on the children's ward.'

Callum left the room without saying another word, and Jade was thankful that he hadn't taken things any further. The mother was upset enough already. She glanced at the boys. They were unusually quiet.

'I'm sorry about the interruption,' she told Alice's mother. Her heart was thumping in response to Callum's silent admonition, but she was becoming more incensed by the minute. What right had he to come storming in here and bawl them out?

'They've always been a handful,' Mrs Sawyer answered wearily, 'and I know they sometimes disturb other people. I know I should sort them out…it's just that I'm so worried about Alice. How long will it take for the test results to come through?' Her face was drawn with anxiety.

'It shouldn't take too long. While we're waiting for them, I'll give Alice broad-spectrum antibiotics intravenously, so that they get to work quickly. As soon as we have the results of the tests, we'll be able to give her a more specific treatment.'

Jacob tugged at her sleeve and asked, 'Is my sister going to be all right?'

'I hope so, Jacob. We're doing everything we can to try to make her better.'

'She's only little,' Matthew said. 'I gived her my teddy bear to cuddle.'

'That was a lovely thing to do.' Jade smiled at both of them. 'I expect your mummy is really pleased to have two boys to help her look after Alice. You know, if Alice sees you two playing quietly together, I think she'll want to get better quickly so that she can join in the fun.'

A few minutes later, when all the procedures had been carried out and she had made sure that Alice was comfortable, Jade left Helen to oversee her patient. Inside, she was still fuming because of Callum's untimely intervention. Did he think she was utterly incapable?

She went over to the desk to write up her chart, and saw that he was coming out of the room next to hers. He walked briskly towards her, and slotted his own chart into the box.

She sent him a frosty stare. Observing her continually was one thing, but embarrassing her in front of a patient was an entirely different matter.

'Have you finished treating your patient?' he asked.

'I have.' She said coolly, 'I'd appreciate it if you wouldn't come barging into my room, laying down the law, when I'm with a patient. It doesn't look good if you come in and undermine my control of the situation.'

'What control was that?'

She glared at him. 'I was perfectly capable of handling things, but I chose to concentrate on my patient, rather than create a fuss. There are far more subtle ways of calming children down, and it was totally unnecessary for you to chastise them and upset the children's mother. She had enough on her plate, without having to listen to you telling her children off.'

He raised a dark brow. 'This, coming from a woman who lets the children in her care run wild? I know things are difficult for you right now, and you do your best in the circumstances, but I hardly think I'm going to be persuaded to change tack on your say-so.'

She narrowed her eyes, incensed by his refusal to accept any blame. 'Who are you to criticise and tell me how to go on? You have no experience of children whatsoever and as far as I'm concerned you have all the sensitivity of a gnat.'

His eyes darkened, and he studied her, his expression brooding. 'Is that so? Don't you think you're being a little *over*-sensitive? You're letting your emotions get in the way of your work. You can't possibly carry out an examination and conduct a conversation with a patient or relative while you're being bombarded with assaults on all sides. I was in the very next room, and I couldn't hear myself think.'

She gritted her teeth. 'I'm sorry that you have trouble handling certain situations,' she said tightly, 'but that isn't my problem. You'll have to find a way of dealing with it, just as I have to adjust to working alongside you. As far as that goes, I'd very much prefer it if you would do me the courtesy of letting me handle my own consultations next time. It's hardly supportive if you come storming in and start laying down the law to the patient's relatives.'

His glance flicked over her. 'I certainly managed to scrape a nerve, didn't I? I had no idea that you were so uptight about working with me. Perhaps your home life is having more of an effect on your outlook than you imagined.'

She glared at him. He was impossible. He was bringing this down to a personal level, whereas she was simply objecting to his high-handed manner. 'I have things to do,' she muttered. 'I don't have time to stand arguing with you.'

She swivelled away from him, her back straight, her shoulders taut with anger, and went and found her next patient. It was only when she managed to calm down a little that it dawned on her that she had actually dared to argue with her boss. A wave of heat ran through her. She had accused him of interfering, of laying down the law. Was she mad? Who, in their right mind, would even think of crossing swords with an acting consultant?

There was no going back now, though, so, instead of dwelling on things, she tried to turn her attention to her work.

It was some time later when she found an opportunity to look in on Alice once more. The little girl was still very poorly, but at least she was less dehydrated, and her fever had subsided a fraction. Her family were gathered around her bedside, and Jade saw that the father was included in the group.

He was holding Jacob on his knee, while Mrs Sawyer was cuddling Matthew. They looked anxious and watchful, but they had been brought together by sudden adversity, and they were as one in their concern for Alice. Seeing them together like this brought a lump to Jade's throat. Putting aside their obvious anxiety, it was the sort of united family life she had always yearned for.

Jade said, 'The test results have come through, and they confirm that Alice has pneumonia. I'm going to add another antibiotic to her treatment regime, and hopefully she'll start to show some signs of improvement from now on. It will take a while for the medication to work, but at least she's stable for the moment, and that's a good sign.'

She left them to watch over Alice and walked back to the desk to look through her charts. Glancing at her, James, the reception clerk, said, 'I've been looking for you. I was off duty yesterday, so I didn't get the chance to tell you, but there was a message from Intensive Care. You remember, you asked me to keep you informed about the man you treated the other day—the subarachnoid haemorrhage?'

'Yes, I remember. Has there been some news?'

He nodded. 'I'm afraid he died in the early hours of yesterday morning. I'm sorry. I didn't get to hear about it myself until I came in to work today.'

A ripple of disbelief ran through her, and she stared at him, her jaw dropping. 'But I thought he was on the mend—last time I checked with the intensive care unit, he was showing some signs of improvement.'

The clerk shook his head. 'Apparently he suffered a stroke. They did what they could for him, but they weren't able to save him in the end.'

Jade stood still for a moment, trying to absorb the news. A cloud of sadness settled on her shoulders. She had hoped so much that he would pull through. 'Thanks for letting me know, James.'

Coming on top of her mishap with the haemothorax patient, this latest blow made her feel even more at a loss. Could she have done any more for the man? Could she have acted any sooner? Perhaps the truth was she was simply no good at her job. She'd had her doubts from the start, and now this looked as though it was confirmation of what she'd known all along. She was inexperienced and liable to make mistakes, and perhaps Callum was right to watch her every move.

'You look unhappy,' a man's voice said, and she looked up to see that Sam was watching her. 'Can I do anything to soothe your troubles away?'

She acknowledged him with a shake of her head. 'I don't think so,' she mumbled. 'I have a lot of things on my mind. I think I just need to be by myself for a while.'

'Is it because I'm a paramedic? Is that why you don't want to know me?'

She stared at him, suddenly jolted into awareness. 'I'm sorry—I'm not sure I know what you mean.'

'I keep trying to ask you out, but I get the feeling that you're trying to avoid me. Is it because I'm not a doctor, or maybe you only go for consultants?'

She sent him a bewildered frown. 'I didn't realise that you were thinking that way. I haven't been trying to avoid you, Sam. I'm always busy here, and just now, with everything that's going on in my life, I don't have time for relationships outside work. It's just the way things are. It's nothing personal.'

He gave her a questioning look, moving in closer to where she was standing by the waiting-room door. 'Are you absolutely sure that you won't change your mind? We could have lunch together some time, couldn't we? Between us, we should be able to work something out.'

She made a weak smile. Most of her lunch-breaks

were taken up with visiting her mother and Gemma. She didn't have time for a private life. 'Like I said, I have—'

'There's a patient coming in—suspected heart attack,' Callum said. 'I need you on board now, Jade.' He sent Sam a cool glance. 'Your partner was looking for you,' he told him. 'Apparently you have another call-out.'

Sam checked his bleeper and shot a look in Jade's direction. 'It looks as though we're both too busy to get together,' he murmured.

She wasn't sure whether Callum had heard that remark, and in theory it shouldn't have mattered. Callum was her boss, and the only worry he had about her conversations with other men was whether they interfered with her ability to do her job.

She sighed inwardly. Why did that bother her? Had she been hoping for some stronger, more personal reaction? That didn't make any sense. After all, she had been annoyed with him for most of the day, one way and another, and now her nerves were snapping, her whole body shaken up and on the alert. It was how she felt most of the time whenever he was around.

Then again, perhaps he was right when he said that with all that was going on in her life right now, she was losing her ability to think straight. She gave a hollow, inward laugh. That was nothing so unusual… Most of the time, as far as Callum was concerned, she was thoroughly confused.

He, on the other hand, let nothing get in the way of his capacity to do his job properly. He was already on his way to meet their patient, and she tried to get her head together and hurried after him.

It was a long day, and she wasn't sorry to see the end of her shift. Back at home, she sent the children out to play, and warned them to stay out of trouble. 'I don't want any more calling out of fire engines or popping next door for food—I just want you to play in the garden until I have your meal on the table, and I want you to stay out of mischief. Can you do that?' Heaven forbid they should cause any more problems with Callum.

Rebeccah nodded, and Connor shifted about as though he was trying to make up his mind.

'Connor?'

He nodded, then shrugged, lifting his shoulders in a restless movement, as though he was anxious to be outside.

'Go on, then.' Satisfied that nothing untoward was likely to happen in the next half-hour or so, she went and changed into clothes that were more casual and comfortable, a soft cotton top and a floaty, pastel-coloured skirt, before making a start on the evening meal. She'd had enough problems for one day, and it was a relief to be home and to have nothing on her mind but preparing a salad.

Glancing out of the French doors to the garden, she saw that the children were giggling, bending down near the fence that divided her property from her neighbour's. She couldn't quite make out what they were looking at, but there were some oddly shaped pebbles spread along the border down there, and they often played with them. Satisfied that nothing was amiss, she went back to washing lettuce leaves under the tap.

Her tranquillity didn't last for long. A few minutes later her front doorbell sounded, and she wiped her hands and went to answer it. If it turned out to be another telephone company salesman who had come to disturb her peace, he would soon find that he had bitten off more than he could chew.

Instead, she was startled to see Callum standing there, and for a moment she simply stood and looked at him.

He was dressed in olive-green chinos and a pale-coloured shirt that was open at the neck, to reveal the lightly bronzed column of his throat. He looked incredibly good and her pulses reacted accordingly, jumping all over the place. She wished he didn't have this effect on her.

'Have I suddenly grown two heads?'

He lifted a dark brow in query and she realised that she had been staring at him.

'Sorry,' she said. 'You took me by surprise.' That was an understatement and a half. Her heart was thumping and she was sure her temperature had shot up several degrees in the last few seconds. She had no idea why she was feeling this way. It was probably nerves. He must have come round because something else had gone wrong.

Then she realised that he was holding something, and when she looked more closely, she saw the kitten nestled in his arms.

'He's a bit wet, I'm afraid,' he said, lifting him up and inspecting him carefully. 'I've dried him off as best I could, but I think perhaps you should keep him inside for a while.'

She stared at him all over again, her heart sinking. What had happened this time? She could have sworn the children hadn't set foot outside the garden. Opening the door wider, she said on a faintly resigned note, 'You'd better come in.'

They went through to the kitchen, and he put Kizzy down in the basket in the corner of the room. 'I think he was after the fish in the pond,' he said, 'but he's obviously not very good at finding them just yet. Either that, or the fish are too quick for him.' He frowned. 'I'm not sure quite how he managed to get into the garden. I thought he was a bit wary of climbing the fence just yet.'

Jade wasn't so sure it had been the kitten's idea. Alarm bells were ringing in her head. At the back of her mind she remembered how the children had been giggling, and she recalled their earlier fascination with Callum's fishpond. It was quite possible that when she had believed they had been innocently playing, they had actually been encouraging the kitten to go through the fence.

'Then again,' Callum murmured, 'I noticed the other day that there's a loose panel lower down. Perhaps he managed to push his way through there. It's quite near the pond.' He frowned. 'I'll have to get it fixed.'

'I'm sorry,' she said. 'One day, though, he's going to be able to scale the fence. He's already testing the boundaries.'

In her mind she was still going over the possibilities of how this had come about. Where the children were concerned, she had a high index of suspicion. It was probably some great plan they had thought up. They had been expressly forbidden from going next door, but this way they probably thought they would have a genuine excuse to go and fetch the kitten back. They'd obviously counted without Callum's swift action.

'Are you all right?' Callum was studying her, trying to gauge her expression.

'I'm fine,' she said. She wasn't going to confide her thoughts with him. No way. He'd already accused her of letting the children run out of control, and after the way he had swept in and sorted out the disruptive element in her treatment room today, she was staying well clear of that area. At least she might be able to get away with this latest escapade. 'I was wondering what you could do to keep the kitten away from the water…for his sake, and for the fish. Is there any way you can screen off the pond?'

'I expect I'll be able to sort something out. Don't worry about it.' He glanced out of the French doors. 'I see your two are having a good time out there. Well, at least, they were. They're heading back towards the kitchen, from the looks of things, and they seem to be a bit subdued.'

Jade wasn't surprised. If she was right, their cunning plan had been thwarted. She said, 'Perhaps they've just realised they've lost Kizzy.'

Rebeccah and Connor came into the room, looking wide-eyed. 'You found him,' Connor exclaimed. 'We was wondering where he was.'

'Did you bring him?' Rebeccah chimed in. 'Was he round your house?'

'He was. I thought you might be worried about him.'

Connor bent down to cuddle the kitten. 'He's wet,' he said, and gave Rebeccah a knowing look.

'Has he been in the pond?' Rebeccah asked.

Callum nodded. 'I'm not sure how it happened.'

'Thank you for bringing him back to us,' Jade said quickly, hoping she could stall the children from blurting anything out. She sent them a warning look and they clamped their mouths shut, looking like a pair of conspirators.

Callum gave her a warm smile. 'You're welcome. I know how fond the children are of him. Besides, I had an ulterior motive for coming around.'

'You did?' She was startled.

He nodded. 'I wanted to come around and apologise to you.'

She frowned. 'I'm not sure that I follow.'

'I was rude earlier today. I was out of order this morning at work.'

Her eyes widened in astonishment. 'You're actually admitting to it?'

He made a brief smile. 'I am. My only excuse is that I was worried about a patient. I'd just spent the better part of an hour trying to save his life, and I had a horrible feeling that I might be losing the battle. The noise from next door was getting to me, but I shouldn't have let rip at you and the people in your treatment room that way.'

'What happened to your patient?'

'I sent him up to Theatre. It looks as though he could be on the mend now.'

'That's a relief.'

'Yes. Anyway, I just wanted to say that I'm sorry for marching in on you.' He glanced around the kitchen and saw her preparations for the meal. 'I can see that you're busy. Perhaps I should get out of your way?'

'It's all right. I was just making supper. It's only salad, but you're welcome to stay and share it with us.'

'I can't, I'm afraid. I have to go out, but I just felt that I should come round and make my peace with you.'

'That's all right. I understand how it must have happened.'

Connor began to tug at Callum's trouser leg. 'Have you two been arguing?'

Callum nodded. 'Sort of.'

'Grown-ups shouldn't argue.' His expression was knowing, making him look older than his years. 'When Rebeccah and me argue, Mummy says, "You should kiss and make up."' He wrinkled his nose. 'Yuck, can you believe it?'

'Your mummy's probably right. Perhaps I should kiss your Auntie Jade? What do you think?'

Rebecca and Connor looked at him wide-eyed. They both nodded.

Callum reached out to Jade, his hands gently clasping her arms. 'From the mouths of babes,' he said. 'I don't think we should disappoint them, do you?'

She wanted to answer, but the words somehow wouldn't come. Her lips were parted in startled wonder, and he took her silence for agreement and gently swooped to claim her mouth. Dazed, she closed her eyes and absorbed the warmth of his kiss, a tender, sweet exploration, as soft as thistledown, as faint as a summer breeze. Her whole body responded, ripples of sheer pleasure running down her spine and seeking out her nerve endings so that even her skin tingled. Heat ran through her veins, and surged through her like a glorious tide.

Then he released her, and she opened her eyes and waited for the world to right itself once more.

'Them kissed,' Connor shrieked, laughing, and Rebeccah smiled, clasping her hands together behind her back.

''Cos you told him to do it,' she said. 'That's why.'

Callum gazed down into Jade's eyes. 'I should leave,' he murmured. 'Things to do, places to go.'

Jade nodded. She was still bemused by that feather-like touch of his lips on hers. For all its lightness she could still feel the imprint of his mouth on hers, like an effervescent trail, as though she had sipped a sparkling wine.

Rebeccah was right, though, wasn't she? It meant nothing, because he had simply responded to Connor's childish demand. Why, then, did she feel so shaken by the experience?

CHAPTER SIX

'Am I going to lose my baby?' The young woman looked at Jade with tear-drenched eyes. 'It's too soon… I know that it's way too soon, but the contractions have started. Please, tell me I'm not going to lose him. He's all I have.'

'We're going to do our very best to look after you and the baby,' Jade told her soothingly. 'You're in shock, and you need to try to relax, Natalie. Keep the oxygen mask over your nose and mouth as much as possible and try not to upset yourself.' That must be easier said than done, she reflected. The poor girl was traumatised, and she was right about the contractions. This baby was on the way, whether they were ready for it or not.

'What's happening here?' Callum asked, coming into the treatment room and glancing at the chart. 'Have you examined the patient?'

Jade nodded and went to speak to him quietly, out of earshot of the girl on the bed. 'She's at around 34 weeks gestation, contractions have started and are getting stronger and more frequent. I'm worried about both her and the foetus. I've made a quick physical examination, and she's bleeding and suffering from uterine pain and tenderness, as well as back pain.'

'Have you called for the obstetrician?'

'I have, yes.'

'Are there any relatives who should be notified…a husband, or parents, perhaps?'

'No husband.' She grimaced. 'Apparently, the boy-friend didn't want to know once she told him that she was pregnant. We're trying to get in touch with her parents.' She shook her head, unable to take in what had brought Natalie here. 'It was a really nasty attack. Who-ever it was who stole her purse used maximum force to make her give it up. She was on an escalator when he pushed her and she fell down the remaining stairs, which has left her with lots of cuts and bruises.'

'She's lucky she isn't in an altogether worse condi-tion, given the circumstances. Are you going to do an ultrasound scan?'

She nodded. 'I was just about to start it.'

'Good. Try to keep your cool.' He gave a brief smile and touched her arm in a light, supportive gesture, and Jade felt her spirits lift. 'Let me know the results. I'll drop by and keep with you on this one. Remember that you should look out for shock and haemorrhaging. A fall like that could have caused the placenta to shear away from the uterine wall—in which case, you need to be on your guard for any sign of foetal distress.'

'I know. I'll do that.' She was glad that he was go-ing to work with her, and as she watched him leave the room she felt a small pang of loss. She couldn't help remembering how it had felt when he had kissed her yesterday at home. It had just been a casual kiss, a gentle brushing of his mouth on hers, and it had meant nothing at all, of course. It had only come about because the children had urged him to do it, but even so, that little glow of wonder was still with her, long after the event.

It wouldn't do her patient any good for her to dwell on any of that, though, and she turned back to her now, setting up an IV line so that she could give Natalie the fluids she needed to replace any blood loss and hopefully counteract the effects of shock.

Helen came to assist, and they both noted that the mother's condition was deteriorating rapidly.

'The foetus is struggling,' Helen said. 'The heart rate is fluctuating and I'm worried about the lack of oxygen.'

Jade nodded. 'We're going to lose this baby unless we do an emergency Caesarean section.' She frowned. 'I'm not sure that we can wait for the obstetrician. Did you page her again?'

'Yes, just a few minutes ago. She'll be down as soon as she can manage it.'

Callum put his head round the door just as Jade was contemplating her next move, and she told him swiftly, 'It isn't easy to tell from the ultrasound scan, but I think there could be a massive haemorrhage where the placenta has abrupted. The foetus is showing signs of distress, and I believe both the mother and the baby are unstable.' She looked at him anxiously. 'I don't know how long it will be before the obstetrician gets here, but it could be too late.'

'Have you ever done a C-section?'

She shook her head. 'I've observed, but I've never actually done one.'

'All right…let's scrub up and I'll talk you through it.'

Her eyes widened. Was she going to be able to do this? Both the mother's and the baby's life depended on her skills as a doctor, and she wasn't at all sure that she was up to it.

In the end, there wasn't any choice but to go ahead with the Caesarean, and she quietly explained to Natalie what they were going to do.

'We have to stop the haemorrhage as quickly as possible,' she said, 'and we're going to have to give you a transfusion to make up for the blood that you've lost. We also need to deliver your baby right now.'

She glanced at Natalie searchingly, giving her time to ask about anything she didn't understand. Natalie looked anxious but didn't interrupt, and Jade went on, 'I'm going to give you an anaesthetic that will ensure you don't feel any pain, but you'll be awake throughout the proceedings, so that you'll be able to talk to us and ask any questions.' She hoped that she sounded calm and in control of the situation.

Helen made things ready for the baby, producing an incubator and making preparations to receive the infant and care for it after the birth.

Callum spoke softly to the young mother-to-be, his whole manner positive and reassuring, and Jade watched him, awed by the calm, gentle way he soothed her. He quietly explained what was going to happen, and told her, 'In just a little while, you should be able to hold your baby.'

Turning to Jade, he said in an undertone, 'Take a few

deep breaths, and calm yourself. Just take it one step at a time. You'll do fine.'

He talked her through the preparations and showed her where to make the incision, and then, a very short time later, she was able to lift the baby from the womb and hand him over to the nurse. The infant was limp and silent and she feared the worst as she clamped the cord, and waited apprehensively as the nurse applied gentle suction to the infant's nose and mouth.

There was still no sound from him, though, and Callum took over, saying under his breath, 'There's no heartbeat.'

He applied his thumbs over the mid-sternum and began compressions, while the nurse made sure that oxygen was readily available. It seemed like an endless wait, and Natalie asked, 'What's happening? Why isn't he making any sound?'

'The doctor's attending to him,' Jade explained. 'Let me check you over for a moment while he makes sure that your son is all right.'

Her patient's blood pressure was low, and Jade checked that the haemorrhage was coming under control before she set about suturing the incision she had made. After a while Natalie appeared to perk up a little, and she said again, 'My baby—what's happening? Please, tell me…is he all right?'

Jade went to check, and just then the baby gave a tremulous cry. Callum wrapped him in a blanket and handed him to his mother, saying softly, 'Do you want to hold your son for a little while?'

Natalie nodded, her eyes devouring the small bundle. She lifted her arms and cradled the infant to her chest, crying quietly.

'Is he going to be all right?' Jade mouthed silently, and Callum inclined his head a fraction.

'I think so. He seems to be responding well enough now. We'll put him into the incubator in a moment, and make sure that he's warm and has an adequate oxygen supply. He's had a rough time of it, poor little fellow, but he's a good enough weight for a pre-term infant. He should do fine.'

Jade was relieved. 'His mother seems to be recovering from her ordeal, which is just as well. I've no idea what can have happened to delay the obstetrician.' She glanced up at him. 'Thank you for letting me do the C-section, and for having confidence in me.'

'You're welcome. After all, you're here to learn, as well as to save lives. It's my job to see that you get the chance to do both.' He smiled at her. 'I think you did really well.'

It was warm praise, coming from him, and Jade basked in the unexpected glow for a moment. Then Katie came into the room and the brief glow of warmth wafted away as she said, 'Jade, there's a suspected heart-attack patient on his way to A and E. Will you take him?'

Jade glanced at Callum, and he nodded. 'I'll finish up here. You go.'

It was an anticlimax, going out of that makeshift delivery room, and her thoughts were still with the mother and baby, but she went to the aid of her new patient and forced herself to concentrate on his problems.

She suspected that Jack Reynolds was suffering from a coronary thrombosis, and after she had examined him and recorded an ECG, she gave him diamorphine to relieve the pain and thrombolytic drugs to dilate the coronary arteries.

When Callum stopped by the door of her treatment room a short time later, Jack was feeling a little better, but he was struggling with his breathing, and Jade was making sure that he was receiving oxygen through a face mask. She checked that the oxygen flow was set correctly, and went to see what Callum wanted.

'I'm going for lunch,' he said, 'and I wondered if I could take you out to eat. I still owe you for the meal the other evening. What do you think? Have you about finished in here? There's a little place not too far from here, and we should have time to relax for a while before we need to get back.'

Coming out of the blue like that, the invitation startled her and her mouth dropped open a little, but she quickly clamped it shut again and said, 'That sounds good. Thanks, I'd like that. Will you give me a few minutes while I write up my notes? I need to find a porter to wheel my patient to the recovery room while we wait for a spare bed in coronary care and then I can temporarily hand him over to Dr Franklin.'

He nodded, and she went to make the necessary arrangements. 'I should speak to the relatives,' she told Dr Franklin, 'but I can't find them anywhere. I was sure that his wife came in with him.'

'She left,' Dr Franklin said. 'The paramedic—Sam— let slip that Mr Reynolds had been with his girlfriend when he was taken ill, and his wife looked as though she had been struck by lightning. Poor Sam didn't know what to do. He hadn't realised the wife had arrived and he tried to cover his mistake, but she didn't want to know any more. I heard her say something about going to her friend's house to collect her children. She said she doubted she would be coming back, and other words that weren't quite as sympathetic, as you might expect.'

Jade winced. Why was it that people couldn't keep faith with one another? So many people were hurt in the process of failing relationships and, most of all, the children were the ones to suffer.

'I hate it when children are involved,' she said. 'It must be so bewildering for them to have their lives torn apart.'

Dr Franklin shrugged. 'That's life,' he said. 'It happens.'

Jade frowned. How could he be so casual about it? It all seemed so unfair. She was still scowling when Callum came and found her, and led her out to the car park.

'What's wrong?' he asked as he helped her into the passenger seat of his sleek silver saloon. He started the engine and turned the vehicle out onto the main road, heading for the outskirts of town. 'Has something happened to your patient?'

'No. He seems to be doing all right.' She sighed. 'I'm trying hard not to judge him, but it isn't easy to treat someone who sees nothing wrong in stamping all over people's feelings. From what I heard, his wife left in floods of tears after learning that he had cheated on her, but he doesn't seem to care at all. He even tried to chat me up once he had started to feel better. Can you believe it?'

He sent her a sideways glance, his mouth curving. 'Actually, I can. You're a beautiful young woman, with a perfect figure, and all that gorgeous honey blonde hair is like a beacon to red-blooded young men. No wonder the male patients and some of the male staff seem to be in a daze whenever you're around.'

She stared at him. 'You're making fun of me. I was being serious.'

'So was I.' He manoeuvred the car on to a country lane and went through the gears. 'I sometimes think you should be wearing a warning label. "Danger…high-voltage female. Risk of heart attack."'

A rush of heat rippled through her. Did he really think she was beautiful? She blinked. 'You're making it up as you go along. I've never seen any of these dazed people.'

'I have. Take Sam, for instance. He can't keep his eyes off you. It's a wonder he ever gets to take any call-outs once he's discovered that you're on duty. His partner has to keep bleeping him.'

'Sam's footloose and fancy-free, and he's an inveterate flirt. At least he isn't married with children.'

Callum didn't answer. They had been driving for about ten minutes, and now Jade saw that they were approaching a lovely little cottage restaurant, bedecked with hanging baskets in full bloom and adorned along the front wall with masses of flowering shrubs. It was set back from the road and backed by rolling hills and lush meadows. Callum drew the car to a halt and they stepped out onto the pavement.

Looking around, Jade could see that sunlight was glinting off the waters of a meandering brook, alongside which ran a dry-stone wall. Overhead, the sky was a clear, vivid blue, and she watched as birds flew down and settled in the nearby trees.

'This is a lovely place,' she murmured.

'I thought you might like it. It's good inside, too.' He placed a hand under her elbow and ushered her inside the old country restaurant, and she tried not to think about the way his gentle touch alerted all her senses and sent them into chaotic disorder. She absorbed the warmth of his nearness and her whole body quivered as his thigh inadvertently brushed hers.

She had to get a grip on herself. It wouldn't do to let her emotions get the better of her, would it? Those things he had said before were not meant to be taken seriously and, when all was said and done, he was still her boss. At work he was ultra-professional, and nothing would stand in the way of getting the job done.

They found a corner table by the window, overlooking the stream where it broadened out into a little pond. Ducks drifted along the surface, diving down into the water every now and again for a morsel of food.

'What would you like to eat?' He handed her a menu, and she studied it briefly, choosing a light salad along with wedges of potatoes and an assortment of creamy dips.

His own meal was more substantial, and he settled for a crusty lattice pie teamed with fresh, beautifully cooked vegetables.

'Has there been any news of your mother and your sister-in-law?' he asked as they started to eat. 'They've both been in hospital for some time now, haven't they?'

She nodded. 'I'm hoping that my mother will be coming home very soon. There were a few problems as she started to heal after the abdominal trauma, but I think she's making headway now. She'll need some help around the house, though, until her shoulder mends, so she'll probably come and stay with me at the cottage for a few weeks.'

'And your sister-in-law? How's she doing?'

'They're worried about complications. Besides the pelvic fracture, some of her underlying organs were injured, so they're taking no chances. They have to be on their guard for any sign of infection. Her head injury has healed, and she seems to be doing a lot better, but it's slow process.'

'Has her husband—your brother—arrived home yet?'

'No, not yet.' She speared a lettuce leaf with her fork, worrying about the delay.

'What's causing the hold-up?'

'I'm not sure. He was in the decompression chamber for a few days after diving to check the pipeline, and then he had to wait for a helicopter to fly him out. There were storms, and that would have delayed him, but I haven't heard from him for the last couple of days.'

'You look as though you're concerned about that.' Callum sipped his iced water. 'Do you think there's a problem?'

'Possibly. Gemma thinks he's reluctant to come home. There are cracks in the relationship and she's worried that he's becoming a stranger to the children. She says she's afraid he doesn't know how to relate to them.'

'They aren't his, are they? Is that the cause of the problem, do you think?'

She shook her head. 'I don't know. He lost his father when he was just a little boy, and I don't think he knows what real family life is like.' She winced. 'Neither of us does.'

Callum gave her a long look. 'It must have been

worse for you in a way. After all, you lost two fathers, didn't you?'

'That's true...but I was older when Ben's father died. I suppose I was more able to handle it then, and anyway there wasn't really any choice. My mother went to pieces and I had to make sure that Ben was all right. It sort of blotted out my own feelings.'

'That's sad.' He signalled for the waitress and ordered desserts for both of them. 'How did you feel when your real father left? You must have been bewildered.'

'I suppose I was at first, but he came back from time to time, and I kept hoping that he and my mother would get back together again. It didn't happen, of course, and my father went to work overseas in the travel industry. When he came to see me he would bring exotic gifts, but what I really wanted was for him to stay home. I pleaded with him not to go away again, but he left, and he never came back.'

She swallowed some of her fruit juice. 'He sent postcards every now and again for a while, but then they stopped coming. I cried myself to sleep at night. I thought I must have been really bad for him to go away and never come back. I thought it was my fault that my parents had split up, and I was sure that he didn't love me anymore. That was why he stayed away.'

'I'm sorry.' He reached across the table and clasped her hand in his, letting the warmth and strength seep into her. She absorbed it like a balm, a potent medicine to shore up her defences.

'It was all a long time ago.'

'Maybe, but it still hurts you, doesn't it? It's an unresolved wound that prods you every now and again, and makes you wary. You're afraid to let your guard down.'

She gave a weak smile. 'Perhaps. It happened so many years ago that it seems foolish to let it go on bothering me.' She straightened, and poised her spoon over her fruit dessert. 'Tell me about your family. Didn't you say that you thought your sister might be pregnant at last?'

He accepted the change of conversation, and began to tell her about his sister's struggle to have a family. She had been married for some time, and now at last she was glowing with the knowledge that she was soon to be a mother.

He paid the bill, and they went outside into the fresh air. The sun was warm on Jade's bare arms, and he draped an arm around her shoulders as they walked along the road a short distance and then crossed over to go and look at the stream. She liked the feel of him close to her, and she was cheered by the warm sense of companionship.

She gazed down at the water. It was clear, and she could see the pebbles that lined the bed of the brook. Small fish darted here and there, and Callum pointed out a duckling that was hiding in the reeds.

'I didn't see him,' she said lightly. 'He was so well hidden. Is he on his own?' She sent Callum an anxious glance. 'I hope his mother is around somewhere.'

Callum laughed softly. 'You can't take on the worries of the world,' he said. 'You'll make yourself a nervous wreck. Anyway, I'm sure she's not too far away.' He looked along the course of the stream. 'Look,' he murmured, 'I expect that's her, coming this way.'

Sure enough, the mother duck paddled by, sweeping up the duckling in her wake. Jade chuckled, and looked up at Callum. His glance slid over her, and in the next moment he had caught her up in his arms and he was kissing her, tasting her lips as though he had been deprived of sustenance for a long, long time.

Jade felt as though her body had turned to flame. His lips trailed fire and she burned for him, wanting the kiss to go on and on, loving the feel of his muscled frame pressuring her soft curves as he leaned into her.

His hands caressed her, stroking along the curve of her spine, spreading out over the swell of her hips. 'Did I tell you how much I've been wanting to do this?' he said, his voice thickened. He drew her even closer to him. 'You tantalise me…you make me want things I've only dreamed of.'

His nearness was doing strange things to her nervous system. Her pulses were leaping, her heart pounding as though it would jump out of her chest, and the deepening fervour of the kiss was taking her breath away.

'You never said,' she managed when his mouth briefly left hers to make a thrilling excursion along the line of her throat.

He lifted his head and made a faint smile. 'There has never been a moment when you were on your own. You always seem to have hangers-on around you…the children, Sam, the whole of A and E.'

'I don't believe a word of it,' she said, giving herself an inward shake. None of this was real. How could it be? He talked of A and E and it all came rushing back to her. He was the consultant. He hadn't even wanted her to work in his department, and as for the children

he had virtually accused her of being incapable of con-
trolling them.

Everything that had happened just now had been
a spur-of-the-moment thing, a sudden whim that was
born on the warm breeze of a summer's afternoon.
She wasn't going to take him seriously. She couldn't,
could she?

A sound in the distance had her turning her head to
see what was coming this way, and her heady world of
dreams tumbled back down to reality as she saw a trac-
tor trundling along the road. Callum saw it, too, and he
reluctantly let go of her, standing back to watch the vehicle make its slow progress along the road.

Callum glanced at the watch on his wrist, and her attention was drawn to the bronze of his skin and the
light covering of dark hair. He was strong and mascu-
line, powerful in his ability to make her go weak at the
knees. She had her work cut out simply trying to keep
her feet on the ground.

'We should be heading back,' he said. 'Our afternoon
stint starts in just a few minutes.'

She nodded. Dreams always came to an end, sooner
or later, and the only difference with this one was that
it had hardly had time to take off.

Back in A and E, she made an effort to smooth over
her tangled emotions, and hurried to check up on her
patients. Jack Reynolds was more comfortable now,
showing signs of improvement, and she checked that his
oxygen intake was sufficient before leaving him to rest.

Natalie, the young mother who had been attacked
and robbed, was waiting to be transferred to the maternity unit.

'How are you feeling?' Jade asked. Natalie's parents were with her, sitting by their daughter's bedside, and Jade was glad to see that the young woman had the support of her family at least.

'I'm much better, thanks.' Natalie looked at the baby, who was in a crib at the side of her bed. 'They say he's going to be all right. I'm so relieved.'

'You've been through a very difficult time,' Jade said. 'You were lucky that the paramedics brought you here so quickly, otherwise there might not have been such a good outcome.'

'I know. They were really good to me.' Natalie smiled. 'Someone from the department store called them, and they were there within a few minutes.' Her expression sobered. 'I just feel so angry that my attacker managed to get away.'

'Let's hope the police will be able to track him down. You never know…they might have caught his image on a security camera.'

'I hope so.'

Jade left Natalie a few moments later, after making sure that both she and the baby were doing well. Things were going much better than she expected at work today, and for once she was pleased with her attempts at getting to grips with A and E.

Going back to the desk to write up her notes, she saw that Callum was coming out of the room where Jack Reynolds was recovering, and her mouth curved in a greeting. The memory of his kisses still lingered, and for all that he might have been caught up in the passion of the moment, back in the country lane, there was no denying that she had been equally ensnared.

She walked over to speak to him, but when she caught sight of his expression, the smile froze on her lips.

'What's wrong? Has something happened to my patient?'

He nodded briefly, his blue eyes cool, like the waters of a lake in winter. 'Have you looked in on Mr Reynolds since you came back from lunch?'

'Yes, I went to check on him as soon as we got back. He was fine. His ECG reading had improved, and I made arrangements to transfer him to the coronary care unit.' She stared at him, her green eyes troubled. 'Has his condition changed? I asked the agency nurse to keep me informed.'

'She would have, but she spoke to me first because she was worried. Just now, as she was making one of her regular observations, she says she found him struggling for breath. Did you check his oxygen?'

'Yes, I did, just a few minutes ago. Everything was working as it should.'

'I don't see how it could have been. The oxygen supply was switched off.'

Jade gasped. 'It isn't possible. I made sure that the valve was open. I don't understand what could have gone wrong.' She was alarmed by this new development. 'How is he now? I must go and see to him.'

'I've already done that, and I've done what I can to make sure that he's comfortable again. You should go and make sure that your notes detail exactly what you did, because his girlfriend is asking questions and wants to know what accounts for his sudden relapse.'

Jade felt the colour drain from her face. 'Should I go and talk to her?'

He shook his head. 'You can leave that to me.' He frowned. 'Fortunately, there have been no serious consequences so far, but this is the second incident where a patient of yours has suffered because the proper procedures don't appear to have been followed. If you say that you did everything correctly, then it looks as though we have a serious problem on our hands. The patient was in no condition to turn off the valve by himself, and neither was the patient with the chest drain able to move the drainage bottle and tube. None of this looks good.'

She looked up at him and moistened her dry lips. 'Do you think I did something wrong?'

His blue glance flicked over her. 'You say that you didn't, and I have to believe you, but I don't have the option of letting the matter rest. Something is wrong here, and I'm in charge, so I have to make sure that whatever is going on is put right.'

'What are you going to do?'

'I'm going to issue a security notice and update the measures we take to ensure patients receive the proper care. We all have to be on alert from here on, and we all have to make sure that we follow correct procedures to the letter.'

She was sure that she had done that, but as Callum strode away, grim-faced and stiff-backed, it seemed all too clear that he had serious doubts about her version of the truth. She didn't know what to do, or how she might put things right, and it was painful to realise that in just a short time their earlier closeness had evaporated into thin air.

CHAPTER SEVEN

'It's all my fault.' The little girl was tearful, her breath coming in short bursts as her asthma attack worsened. 'I spilled something on Daddy's computer…and now it won't work.' She paused to get her breath, but Jade could see that it was becoming more and more difficult for the child to get air into her lungs.

'Don't worry about it, Sarah,' Jade said soothingly, concerned that the five-year-old was becoming more and more agitated by the minute. 'Accidents happen sometimes, and I know you didn't mean to do any damage. You need to just try to settle down and relax. Do you want to cuddle teddy for a while? He needs a friend to hold him.'

She wanted to distract the little girl, but the child was too upset for that to work. 'But Daddy shouted at me…' She gulped, trying to suck in a breath, 'And then Mummy shouted at Daddy.' Her breathing was fast and jerky, and when Jade checked her pulse it was way too fast.

'I'm sure no one's cross with you now, and your mummy and daddy just want you to get well again.' She was becoming very anxious about this little girl. Her lips were showing signs of cyanosis, and that meant there wasn't enough oxygen circulating in her blood. Very soon she would be exhausted, and Jade was afraid that her consciousness level would fall.

She gently helped the child to breathe the nebulised oxygen and salbutamol that would alleviate her symptoms, but as the girl's condition continued to deteriorate she set up an intravenous line so that she could give her steroids.

'I'm going to give her aminophylline,' she told the nurse who was assisting, 'and then we'll set up a maintenance infusion. We had better send for the paediatrician.'

Callum came to stand alongside her and watch the proceedings. 'You should call for the anaesthetist as well. We may need to intubate if her condition gets any worse.' He glanced around. 'Are the parents not here?'

'They're in the waiting room,' she told him in a low voice. 'They were arguing and their attitude to one another was making Sarah upset and causing her breathing difficulty to worsen, so I didn't want to allow them in just yet.'

He gave a slight frown, and she started to worry all over again. Did he think that was the wrong course of action? Since the problem with the heart patient the other day, she had found it hard to know what he was thinking. He had kept his distance and only acted in a coolly professional manner towards her, and it was such a contrast to the way he had been with her at the restaurant. She was bewildered and uncertain now where he was concerned. 'I thought perhaps just the mother could come in, initially, once I've managed to stabilise the child. On her own, she might be able to calm her daughter.'

'That sounds like a good compromise.' He looked over the child's chart. 'If she continues to go downhill, you could add ipratropium to the nebuliser. It's a bronchodilator, and it should help. Repeat the dose six-hourly until you see an improvement, and in the meantime arrange for her to be admitted to the paediatric ward.'

'I will.' Despite her reservations about him, she was glad of his intervention. There was nothing more upsetting than seeing a child struggle for breath and to feel that there was nothing you could do to improve the situation. With Callum to back her, she felt that the little girl would have the best chance possible to get well. As a doctor, he was among the best, and she was in awe of his skill and knowledge.

In between dealing with her other patients, she watched over the child for the rest of the day, until a bed was found for her on the children's ward.

'She seems to be breathing a little more easily now,' she told the anxious parents. 'The medication seems to be working. You'll need to make sure that she stays calm and untroubled, though, or she might start to suffer more difficulties.'

'We'll remember that,' the father said. 'I should never have lost my temper the way I did. I didn't know that it would have such a bad effect on her.'

'It wasn't entirely your fault,' Jade said quietly. 'She was suffering from a chest infection, too, and that was probably the main problem in the beginning. I think we have that under control now, though.'

'Thanks for all your help,' Sarah's mother said.

Jade smiled. 'You're welcome.'

At home that evening, things were not going too well with Connor. 'Why hasn't my daddy come home?' he said. 'I talked to him on the phone and he said he was coming to see us, but he didn't. He was lying.' His lips clamped together in a pout. 'He doesn't love us any more.'

Jade gave the boy a cuddle. 'He loves you loads and loads,' she told him, 'and he loves Rebeccah, too.'

The little girl looked worried, and Jade put her arm around her, too. 'Your daddy's working a long way away, and sometimes it isn't easy for him to get back home as soon as he would like. I'm sure he wants to be with you both.'

'Why hasn't he phoned us again?' Rebeccah asked. 'I don't think he wants to talk to us.'

'I don't know why he hasn't phoned,' Jade said, 'but I do believe that he would talk to you if he could. We just have to wait a little longer to find out what's happening.'

Jade was worried about the lack of contact, too, and she was concerned that she hadn't been able to get through to the rig when she had put in a call. Had something happened to prevent Ben from coming home?

The children went out into the garden to play with the kitten, and Jade hoped that she had done enough to soothe their worries for the time being. She set about making some inroads into her chores, checking on the children from time to time, and a while later she went outside to bring them in.

'It's time to get ready for bed,' she called out to them. They were standing by the wrought-iron gate, and they both turned as she approached. 'We're talking to Callum,' Rebeccah said, her voice tinged with excitement. 'He said he'll take us to the Castle fête.'

'It's tomorrow,' Connor put in. 'It's next to the castle and there's a motorbike show and rides. It'll be well good.'

Jade frowned. She didn't want to dampen their enthusiasm, but this was the first she'd heard of it. 'I'm not sure about that,' she said. 'I don't know anything about this fête.'

'But it's Saturday tomorrow, and there's no school,' Rebeccah said. 'Please, can we go?'

By now Jade had reached the gate, and she saw that Callum was standing there on the other side. He was dressed in smart chinos and a dark blue shirt that contrasted well with the light bronze of his skin, but she tried not to dwell on how good he looked. It was altogether too disturbing. He was holding a pair of secateurs, and it looked as though he had been pruning back an overgrown shrub that was trailing branches across the gate.

'What's this about taking the children to a fête?' Jade asked.

'I didn't actually say that we would definitely go there,' he told her, his gaze flicking over her, taking in the snug fit of her cotton top and lingering momentarily on the way her jeans moulded the gentle curve of her hips. 'I said that we would have to ask you if it would be all right. From what they've been telling me, I think they're both feeling a little down just now, and it might be just the thing to cheer them up.'

He snipped a couple more stems and then stood back to survey his handiwork. 'That should do it,' he murmured. He glanced at her. 'What do you think?'

She frowned. 'I think the shrub looks just fine,' she said.

His mouth made a crooked line. 'I meant, what do you think about the trip to the castle? We're both off duty tomorrow, aren't we? And it looks as though the weather's going to stay bright, so we could make a day of it. I know that you would like to go and see your mother and Gemma first thing, but I could pick you all up after that…say around eleven o'clock?' He raised a questioning brow.

Jade thought it over. The children were watching her eagerly and she didn't want to let them down. 'I suppose that would be all right.'

Rebeccah and Connor whooped with joy, and seeing their joyful faces more than made up for the shock of having this outing sprung on her out of the blue.

'That's good. It's all settled, then.' Callum smiled at the children.

Jade wasn't so sure that this was anything to celebrate. Had she really just committed herself to a whole day in Callum's company? Working with him was one thing, but this was entirely different… She wasn't quite sure how to separate out the individual parts—the professional relationship, which wasn't always straightforward, and the one they shared outside the hospital.

Callum didn't make things any easier, did he? He tended to blow hot and cold, being fairly relaxed with her away from the hospital but maintaining a professional distance in the A and E department. It was confusing, to say the least.

The children were bubbling over with excitement at the prospect of a day out, though, and the next morning, when the time came to set off for the castle, they were in high spirits.

'Hurry up, Auntie Jade. Let's go…now.' They were impatient to be off, but Jade still had to load things into the boot of Callum's car…spare sets of clothes in case of accidents, first-aid kit, drinks bottles and numerous other bits and pieces. Jade was sure Callum would come to regret his offer before the day was out. He had never had much to do with children, and he probably didn't have any idea how wearing it could turn out to be. She had already found out to her cost that they had far more energy than she had.

It was a beautiful, cloudless day, though, and when they arrived in the castle grounds, the children were fascinated by the grandeur of the stately home and the myriad things on display.

'Shall we go and take a look at the stalls first?' Callum suggested to them. 'The motorbike display starts in an hour, so that will give you some time to have a go on some of the rides, or try your luck at winning something.'

He seemed to be totally at ease, and Jade slowly began to relax. She helped Connor to hook a plastic frog from a swirling watercourse, and Callum showed Rebeccah how to fire corks at cardboard cut-outs in a mock-up display and make water shoot from their spouts.

By the time they sat down on the terraced seating area to watch the motorbike display, Connor had won a plastic sword and shield from the hook-a-frog stall, and Rebeccah was hugging a fluffy teddy bear.

The motorbike riders put on a spectacular effort and Jade chuckled as they made some comic forays around the grassed arena. They were arranged in pairs, riding their bikes side by side, and joined hands as they went, stretching far apart and coming together at the last minute, and throughout the presentation a clown topped the three tiers of acrobatic bikers, performing antics to make the audience howl with laughter.

'It's good to see you relax and laugh,' Callum said, giving her a sideways glance. 'You've had a lot to cope with lately, and I think you needed a break.'

She smiled at him. 'You're probably right. I've been so busy trying to hold everything together that I haven't had time to wind down. I haven't been used to looking after children, and it's been a bit of a learning curve for me, to be honest.'

'I think you've done well.' He made a wry face, and his eyes were glinting with humour. 'Even I can see that they can be a handful. I've had even less experience of it than you, but I know it hasn't been easy. You've had to cope with A and E as well, and that must have been difficult.'

She sent him a quick look, her expression serious. 'I haven't always managed as well as I'd hoped. I knew that working in Emergency would be tough, and it's certainly hard when you lose a patient or when you're faced with a child who is in immediate danger. I think I'd expected to feel all those kinds of reactions, but I wasn't prepared for the other happenings…causing a patient distress because of the wrong positioning of the drainage tube or the oxygen valve being switched off.' She frowned. 'It makes me look as though I'm not competent, not able to do my job properly, but I felt sure that I'd done everything correctly.'

'It was lucky that the nurses noticed what had happened. No real harm was done in the end.'

'But it could have been bad, couldn't it, if no one had noticed?' She shook her head. 'It makes me begin to doubt myself even more. I didn't have a lot of confidence to begin with, but these events are making me uncertain, making me unsure of myself. I'm almost afraid to act on my own initiative in case something goes wrong.' She threw him a troubled glance. 'I know that you've started to question whether I'm up to the job.'

'I didn't say that.'

'You didn't have to. I saw it in the way you behaved towards me afterwards. You were remote and cool, and I felt as though my abilities were being weighed in the balance.'

'I don't think that's the truth of the situation. You're probably overreacting because you felt that the onus was on you, but no one is accusing you of anything. If I seemed distant, it's because I have to take responsibility for what goes on in the department. I'm the acting consultant, and I have to be mindful of my obligations to the patients as well as to the staff. It throws everyone off balance when something like that happens. You have to question what's going on.'

She wasn't certain how to take his words. On the one hand he was telling her that she wasn't being blamed for what had happened, but on the other there was no admission from him that he had faith in her.

He slid an arm around her shoulders. 'I think you should try to forget about work for now. Try to relax and simply enjoy the day for what it brings.'

Maybe he was right, and she should try to do as he said. He was holding her in a way that offered comfort, and she wanted to be able to lean back and let her troubles drift away. Would he be there to support her?

They bought lunch from the refreshments tent and sat at a table on the open grassed area, where they could watch the children run and play. Rebeccah and Connor were having a wonderful time, and Connor was waving his sword at all and sundry and making friends with other little boys nearby. Rebeccah sat with another little girl and they giggled about pop stars and dance moves, joining in with the lyrics as the nearby rock band belted out lively music to entertain the crowd.

Callum studied the programme of events while Jade sipped her iced drink. The sun was warm on her bare arms and on her legs and she leaned back in her chair and let the gentle rays warm her through and through.

'There's a dog show later this afternoon,' he said. 'Apparently they have to negotiate an obstacle course and see who does it in the quickest time. Then there's a mongrel event, where the dogs are let loose to see if they can catch a fake hare. I expect the children will love all that.'

'I imagine they will.' She studied him from under her lashes. He was settling into this day out as though it was something he had done many times before, and she felt a tingle of admiration for him, and gratitude for his generous actions. She said, 'It was good of you to arrange all this. I know Connor was unhappy, and this has been the best medicine in the world for him.'

'I'm happy that they're both having a good time.' His gaze travelled over her. 'I think it's what you needed, too. You're overdue for a break.' He reached for his drink and took a long swallow, and she watched the movement of his throat with fascination, before letting her glance settle on his long, capable fingers as they circled his glass. 'Besides,' he said, 'I'm actually having a good time.' He chuckled. 'It's a great experience, spending time with a sweet, attractive girl and watching her melt in the sunshine.'

She tossed a plastic cup at him and wiped the faint beads of perspiration from her brow with the back of her hand. 'You're right, I'm decidedly sticky, but you don't go around telling a girl that.'

He laughed. 'Perhaps we should take these two off to the bouncy castle. Hopefully, they can get rid of some of their energy over there.'

Connor made swashbuckling noises and slashed the air with his sword as they walked across the field, while Rebeccah did her best to avoid the swipes when they came her way.

Jade made sure that they were happily settled on the bouncy castle before she stepped back to watch them. It was good to see them having fun.

'Do you think you'll want to have children of your own one day?' Callum asked, coming to stand next to her and sliding an arm around her waist. 'You seem to be happy, taking care of them, despite all the hassles you've been through.'

She thought about that for a moment or two. It was distracting, having his arm around her that way, his hand resting lightly on the rounded swell of her hip. She was conscious of his thigh brushing against her, and it made her head swirl, and she found herself wondering what it would be like to have his children. It was sheer madness to think that way. Maybe it was just the heat that was making her feel light-headed.

'I think I would like a family of my own,' she said, at last, evading his glance, 'but I'm not sure that it will happen. I don't think I would ever be able to find a man that I trust enough to father my children. I'd need to know that he was going to stay around long enough to see them through to adulthood, but there are never any guarantees about that, are there?' She winced. 'Gemma's first husband didn't stay around, and now she has doubts about my brother's commitment.'

'It isn't Gemma's experience that's filling you with doubts, though, is it?' He tucked a hand under her chin and lifted her head so that she had no choice but to look into his eyes. 'It's the fact that your father left you when you were little…that's why you're reluctant to get deeply involved with any man. I've sensed it for some time now. It's the reason you get upset with the male patients who are less than perfect. You've grown a shell around yourself to protect yourself from being hurt, but you'll never learn to trust yourself to someone else until you resolve the problem of your father.'

'I don't know. Perhaps you could be right.' She made a negligent shrug. 'I try not to think about it.'

'Because it still hurts.' He tilted his head until his eyes were on a level with hers. 'Am I right?'

'Maybe.'

He ran his thumb lightly over her cheek. 'If you were to find him again, you might be able to ask him the questions you've kept hidden inside yourself for all this time.'

'That might not do me any good. He might tell me that I was right all along, and that he never cared for me.'

'He might…but then you would know for certain, and you would be able to put it behind you and move on. You could do something with your life and have more confidence in yourself. As things are now, you can't be sure why he left and never came back, and you're in a kind of limbo, and you're full of doubts and uncertainties. Only he can resolve them for you.'

'That may be so, but I'm not going to take time out to look for him,' she said. 'He left me and my mother and I feel bitter about that, it's true, but, no matter what you say, I can't bring myself to waste time searching for him.'

He slid both hands around her waist and drew her to him. 'Would you allow me to go ahead and search for you?'

She shrugged again. 'I don't know… I suppose so.' It was almost impossible for her to think clearly while he was holding her this way. The touch of his hands burned through the fabric of her clothes and seared her flesh as though it had turned to flame.

She gave herself an inward shake and tried to clear her head. 'I doubt that you'll be able to find him, anyway. He was working as a guide for a travel company that specialised in adventure holidays. He would take people on safari, through the desert or on jungle treks. I don't know if he's still doing that. My mother tried getting in touch with him after he left, but there were no letters from him.'

'It gives me somewhere to start, anyway.' He looked down at her. 'Do you think your mother will have any problem about us contacting him again?'

'I doubt it. She was over him a long time ago, and

the only reason she ever spoke about him was to try to make things easier for me.' She made a grimace. 'I'll tell her that you're thinking of seeking him out, and see what she says.'

'That's good.' He smiled. 'Trust me, I think it will be good for you to resolve this once and for all.'

He turned to greet the children who were coming down off the bouncy castle, and she studied him surreptitiously. Why was he prepared to do this? Was it because he cared for her, just a little? She might have asked him, but a part of her was afraid that he would laugh it off and simply say that he was doing it because he wanted her to have a clear head for her work and more confidence to act alone.

They went to watch the dog show and a performance from a marching band, and by late afternoon they were ready to return home. The children were tired but happy, and as they piled out of the car and headed towards the cottage door, Connor said, 'Can we go there again one day?'

Jade gave him an affectionate smile as she unlocked the front door. 'I should think so. You had a good time, then?'

Connor nodded. Callum was bringing up the rear, laden with bits and pieces from the boot of his car, and he asked, 'What did you like best, Connor? What is it that makes you want to go back? Was it the motorbike display, or the marching band? Or was it the dog show? You loved that, didn't you?'

'It's 'cos I want to get another sword and shield,' Connor said. He swished the sword in the air. 'I love it.' He was still slicing the air as he ran with Rebeccah towards the kitchen.

Jade chuckled. 'So much for travelling fifty-odd miles. I could have taken him to the local toy shop if that was all he wanted.'

Callum shook his head, stifling a laugh. 'And so much for broadening their minds with new experiences. There's just no competition when you're up against a plastic sword, is there?'

He put the bags down on to the nearest table and Jade glanced from the hallway into the kitchen. 'Rebeccah's introducing Kizzy to the teddy bear and Connor's fighting an invisible assailant. They're both hyped up.' She turned around to smile at him. 'Thanks for taking us out. It was a lovely day.'

He reached for her, tugging her towards him. 'I'm glad you had a good time. I thought it was great. I'm almost sorry it had to come to an end.'

'Would you like something to drink? I could put the kettle on.'

'Maybe. In a moment.' He bent his head towards her. 'There's something I've been wanting to do all day…' He captured her mouth with his, and steadied her against the wall. 'You taste like strawberries,' he murmured. 'Strawberries and ice cream.'

'That sounds about right,' she mumbled against his lips. 'I finished off Connor's dessert for him.' His kiss was doing strange things to her insides, filling her veins with effervescence and switching her pulses to overdrive, so that her legs were getting weaker by the second.

'You're delicious,' he said, his voice roughened, 'and I think I want to devour you bit by bit… Or maybe I should just lick the cream from your sweet flesh.' His tongue slid down the column of her throat and dipped to travel along the fullness of her breast as he nudged the opening of her cotton top to one side. 'You're exquisite,' he murmured, and then sighed huskily. 'What am I to do? I can't get enough of you.'

She might have answered, if she could have summoned her voice from the depths of dreamland, where she was drifting away on a cloud of happiness, but then a clatter from the kitchen brought her shockingly back to earth.

'What was that?'

Callum turned his gaze towards the kitchen. 'The kitten just missed being slain by the fiendish warrior. He made his escape over the kitchen worktop and your baking dish has taken a dive.'

She closed her eyes briefly and leaned back against the wall. 'I should go and sort them out.'

He nodded and gave a heavy sigh. 'Perhaps I'll forgo the tea. I've just remembered some papers I need to sort through. I'm supposed to be doing a presentation on emergency management in the hospital lecture room next week. I'd better go and make a start on it.'

Jade sent him a bemused look. Was he being serious? How could he turn from ardent love-making one minute to hospital presentations the next? Then she heard the sound of the children squealing in the kitchen, and it all made sense.

He'd had enough of family life. Making love to her was an opportunistic thing, and he didn't want to stay around now that it was out of the question. He had put himself out for Connor's sake, and Rebeccah's, and perhaps making out with their aunt had been the icing on the cake. Now that he had done all he could, there was no point in hanging around.

She straightened up. 'All right,' she said. 'If you're sure.' She went and opened the front door and stood to one side to let him leave. 'Thank you again for today.'

Perhaps her voice sounded a little stilted, or maybe something else had alerted him, but he gave her an odd, quick look.

'Do you want me to stay and help out?' he asked.

She shook her head. 'No. I'll be fine, thanks.'

'I'll probably not be around tomorrow,' he said. 'I promised I would go to a family gathering, so it looks as though I'll see you back at work on Monday.'

'That's OK.' She watched him go, and felt a huge emptiness settle in the pit of her stomach. More than anything, she wanted him to stay, but she wasn't going to plead with him and lose her sense of pride. What was the matter with her? Was she falling in love with him? Was that why she felt this way, as though she was suddenly lost and alone, tossed adrift because he wasn't going to be there for her?

CHAPTER EIGHT

'DADDY, Daddy! Where was you? Why didn't you come home?' Connor flung himself at Ben and gripped him tightly round the legs.

Ben hugged him. 'I tried to get here sooner, son, but there was something wrong with the helicopter and we had to wait for it to be fixed.'

'Couldn't they get another one?' Rebeccah asked.

'Yes, but then there was an explosion on the rig and we all had to help get people to hospital.' He lifted Rebeccah into his arms and kissed her. 'I would have come home sooner if it had been possible, sweetheart.'

He looked at Jade, his grey eyes apologetic. 'I couldn't even phone to let you know what was happening because the phone line was down. I'm sorry. I didn't mean to worry anyone.'

'At least you're home now,' she said, giving him a hug. 'We've missed you.'

'Me, too.' Ben smiled and looked at Rebeccah and Connor. 'I've brought you a present each. Go and look in my holdall.'

The children scooted off, and when they were out of

earshot Jade asked anxiously, 'What's this about an explosion? Were you hurt? What about the other men on the rig?'

'There were three casualties who had to be airlifted out, and they're doing all right now. I was lucky…I only suffered a minor burn to my leg. I'm just thankful that the explosion was limited to one small area, and that it happened at night when there was only a skeleton staff on duty. It could have been much worse, otherwise.'

'I'm just relieved to have you home safe and sound, and Gemma will be over the moon.' She looked at her tall, dark-haired brother, and felt a rush of affection for him. 'Have you come straight here from the airport?'

He shook his head. 'I went to see Gemma and Mum first. I thought I would stay with the children for a while and see them off to bed, and then go back to the hospital, if that's all right with you?'

'Of course it is. I'm glad you went there first. How are they doing?'

'Mum's OK. She said they might send her home tomorrow or the day after, but I expect you know that.'

Jade nodded. 'She mentioned it this morning when I went to visit. They have to wait until tomorrow to confirm it when the consultant does his round. Things came to a bit of a halt over this weekend because her doctor wasn't on duty. What about Gemma? She must have been thrilled to see you.'

He winced. 'I'm not so sure about that. Yes, she was startled, and pleased to begin with, but she has this hang-up about me being away so much of the time, and we sort of struggled to get through that. She thinks I don't want to be with them. I don't think she's ever been used to me working on the rigs.'

'It doesn't fit in very well with family life, does it? I know the children miss you.'

'I know it isn't the ideal solution, but I wanted to earn good money so that we could have a better future together. Anyway, Gemma always says I disrupt things when I come home. She just gets used to me being around and changing her routine, and then I have to go away again. I sometimes think she would prefer it if I were to stay away.'

Jade shook her head. 'I know that isn't true. She loves you and she wants you to stay home and perhaps do a different kind of job. The money isn't that important to her. A proper family life is what Gemma wants most of all.'

'I don't know about that. I'm not really skilled at anything else. This is what I've always done.'

'It doesn't mean you have to do it for the rest of your life, though, does it? As it is, you're missing out on the children growing up.' She glanced at him. 'Perhaps you're not bothered about that. After all, you never had a father to be there for you.'

He looked as though he was stunned for a moment. 'Of course I want to see them growing up, but I need to provide for them. I haven't been doing any of this just for myself.'

'Perhaps you should tell Gemma that.'

'I have. It doesn't seem to make any difference.' He sighed. 'She's not well and she's out of sorts, so it's probably the wrong time to be going over old ground. I'll just try to cheer her up the best way I can.' He gave a quick smile. 'Thanks for looking after the children while she's been out of action. We both appreciate what you've done…' He broke off as the children came back with their parcels, shaking them to see if they could guess what was inside, and then they all went into the kitchen to have supper and talk about all that had been going on while he was away.

'I've got a fire station,' Connor whooped. 'Look, Auntie Jade.' His face said it all. Rebeccah tore the wrapping paper from her gift and gazed at it in wonder. 'It's a baby dolly, and she drinks milk. She's lovely. Isn't she lovely, Auntie Jade?'

'She is,' Jade agreed. 'You both have lovely presents.' She only wished that Ben and Gemma could be as happy and sort out their marriage problems. Seeing the way the children had greeted Ben when he had first arrived just went to show how much they loved him. He might not be their real father, but he was everything they wanted.

It was hard work, getting the children to settle into bed that night, but Ben stayed with them until they went to sleep, and then he set off for the hospital once more.

Jade realised things were likely to be chaotic for a while, now that Ben was home, but between them they would find a way to manage things.

At work next morning, she ran into Sam as he was speaking into his radio by the ambulance. He lifted a hand in greeting as she was about to go into A and E, then signalled for her to wait a moment.

'We've just dropped someone off here,' he said, cutting the call, 'and now we have to go to a man who's collapsed with abdominal pains, so I can't stop to talk.

I just wanted to ask what happened with the girl we brought in from the department store the other day. Is she all right? Did she manage to keep her baby?'

Jade nodded. 'She's been transferred to the maternity unit. The baby was born prematurely, but he's doing fine, from what I've heard.'

'That's good.' Sam was relieved. 'I felt so sorry for her when we found her at the bottom of the escalator. All she asked about was her baby.'

'It was a horrible thing that happened to her. I just hope they find the man who did it.'

'They did. I heard that some people in the store collared him and stopped him from leaving. Apparently the police have him in custody now. He was wanted for other offences.'

'I'm glad they've caught him.'

'Me, too.' Sam climbed into the front of the ambulance, waving as he and his partner started to drive away, and Jade continued on into A and E.

'Jade, there you are. I've been looking for you...' Callum said. 'Do you have a moment?'

Jade was confused. 'I'm not late,' she said, glancing at her watch. Had he seen her talking to Sam and decided to take her to task about it?

He smiled. 'I know that. Why do you go straight into guilt mode?' He studied her for a moment, shaking his head, and then drew her to one side, out of the way of the main doors. She tried not to let the sudden leap of her pulses throw her off track. He was somehow too close all at once, altogether too vibrant and overpoweringly male. He said quietly, 'I just wanted to say that your mother is down here.'

Jade's eyes opened wide in shock. 'Down here? Is she ill? How can that have happened? Why aren't they treating her on the ward?'

'No…no, it's nothing like that. She was going along to your sister-in-law's ward, but she came out of the lift on the wrong floor and then struggled to find her way. I think usually someone pushes her there in a wheelchair, but today she wanted to try walking there on her own. I've sat her down in the waiting room because I thought you might want to take her up to see your sister-in-law yourself. She's OK, but she does look a little frail.'

'Oh…I see.' She waited for her heart rate to settle down, and then added, 'Thanks for looking after her. I'll go and have a word.' She gave him a quick smile. 'She can be quite an independent soul when she wants, but I'm glad she thought to come down here.'

He nodded. 'You're right there. It sounds to me as though it's a case of like mother, like daughter. You can't be self-sufficient all the time. In some instances, you just have to rely on other people to help out.'

'Maybe.' It was good in theory, but in her experience it didn't always work out that way. Sometimes there *was* no one around to lend a hand.

She went and found her mother in the waiting room, and together they made their way up to Gemma's ward. 'It's good to see you up and about, Mum,' Jade said. 'Does it mean that you're feeling a little better?'

'I am.' Her mother's fair curls danced as she nodded her head. 'The doctor came to see me first thing this morning, and he says that if the lab results come back as he expects, I can go home tomorrow.'

'That's great news. The children will be really happy to see you.'

'I can't wait.' Her mother sent her a sideways glance. 'I was very impressed with that young man who showed me into the waiting room. He seems really nice. I told him that I was lost, and that when I saw the sign for A and E I thought I'd come and find you and see if you could help out, and he was so kind. He didn't dismiss me as some kind of ditherer, or send me off with someone else to guide me. He said we would wait for you to arrive, and he went and brought me a cup of coffee and sat and chatted with me for a while. He lives next door to you, doesn't he?'

'That's right…he's my landlord.'

'Yes, I remember. I think you thought that might be a problem, but he told me about the things the children get up to, and we had a laugh. He's lovely.'

'He can be…' Jade looked at her mother and noticed the colour warming her cheeks. Callum was obviously a better tonic than all the medicine the hospital had to offer.

'Don't you get on well with him?' Her mother's green eyes were all-seeing. 'Is it difficult for you because he's your boss?'

Jade said cautiously, 'I think it's just a strange situation for me. He's very good at what he does, and the work is important to him. He takes his responsibilities seriously and I think he's a brilliant doctor. It's outside of work that things get a little unsettling, and I'm never quite sure of myself around him.'

'That's a shame.' There was a twinkle in her mother's eyes. 'I had the idea that you two might make a lovely couple. Was I so far out in my judgement?'

Jade grimaced. Over these last couple of weeks she had been drawn to Callum and had even dared to dream that something might come of it, but now… Now she was confused. She couldn't be sure that he felt the same way, and she was desperately afraid of being hurt. She didn't want to put her trust in him and then be let down.

'Yes, I think perhaps you were.' She sent her mother a fleeting glance. 'Actually, he seems to think that I have problems…ones that go back as far as my childhood. Mostly that I haven't got over my father leaving us, and also the fact that we never heard from him again. He thinks if I were to confront my dad and ask him why he broke off all contact, things would start to get better for me.'

Her mother thought about that for a moment. 'You know, he's probably right. You were devastated when your father left and didn't come back, and it was even more traumatic for you when your stepfather died. You seemed to handle it well enough at the time, but that was only because I crumpled and you tried to stay strong for Ben. I think you were so used to bottling up your feelings that it became a way of life, and you've learned that people you love don't stay around.'

'I don't know. You could be right, I suppose.' They reached the door to Gemma's ward and Jade stopped for a moment and said, 'So, you wouldn't have any objection if we were to find out what happened to my dad? It wouldn't hurt you if we discovered that he simply lost interest?'

'No, Jade, it wouldn't upset me. I had the love of your stepfather to restore my faith in men, and his is the memory I will always cherish.'

'That makes me feel better. I'm glad.' They walked onto the ward and went to find Gemma, and Jade stopped for a moment or two to say hello, before hurrying back to A and E. A nurse promised that she would make sure her mother returned safely to her own ward.

'She's with Gemma, then?' Callum asked as Jade walked into the department. He was supervising the transfer of a patient to Theatre, and Jade waited while the patient's trolley was wheeled into the lift.

'Yes, she's with Gemma.' She checked her list of patients and reached for a chart. 'Thank you for letting me take her up there, and for looking after her while she was waiting for me. I must say you made a wonderful impression on her. She was singing your praises all the way.'

He smiled. 'She's a lovely lady. I enjoyed talking to her.'

His smile lit up his face and Jade forgot herself for a moment, fascinated by the way his mouth curved and by the soft play of light over his features. He had a strong jaw and compelling eyes, eyes that made you want to drown in those blue depths.

'Jade?'

'Sorry… Yes, I think so, too.' She tried to pull herself together. There was simply no way she should be letting herself fall for him. He was her boss, her landlord, and it was hardly a mutual admiration pact that they shared. Half the time he thought her head was in the clouds, that she was so busy with looking after Gemma's children and worrying about her mother and sister-in-law that she wasn't able to concentrate on her job. No wonder he had thought she needed a break.

And, anyway, he'd engineered that for the children initially, not for her.

'Is there something on your mind?'

'Er…no.' She averted her eyes from his keen gaze. 'I meant to ask if you managed to sort out your presentation the other day. You had to leave fairly suddenly on Saturday to go and work on it, didn't you?'

'That's right. It was the baking tin that reminded me.'

She risked a glance at him. 'That seems like an odd reminder.'

'Yes, it does, but when the kitten knocked it over it made me recall my mother's baking sessions, and that made me think of the family gathering at my parents' place. It was their anniversary yesterday, and they wanted the whole family there for most of the day because it was a kind of treble celebration…one for the anniversary, another for my sister becoming pregnant after a long struggle and another for my brother, who has just announced that his wife is expecting a baby, too.'

'Oh, I see… So that was good news all round, then? I thought it might have been an excuse for—'

He frowned. 'Excuse?' He stared at her. 'For leaving early, you mean?'

Jade was beginning to wish that she hadn't blurted out her innermost thoughts. 'Well…of course you had things to do, and children can be a pain when you're not used to them, can't they?' There was no way she wanted him to put two and two together and realise that she had wanted him to stay and hold her and kiss her some more.

'The children were great. They weren't a minute's

trouble. We may even have reached a kind of under-standing.' He was smiling once more, and Jade was faintly relieved that he hadn't picked up on her main concern.

'There's a patient coming in,' Helen said, coming to-wards them. 'Late forties…a man with abdominal pains. Sam says the pain appears to be poorly localised, and there's been nausea and vomiting.' She checked the chart. 'There's a history of cardiac disease.'

'We'll take him,' Callum said. He turned to Jade and added, 'You can lead on this one. It'll be good practice for you.'

Jade grimaced. She was more than a little apprehen-sive as she hurried to meet her patient. Abdominal pains could present as a symptom in a variety of illnesses, in-cluding appendicitis, bowel obstruction or renal cal-culi. She was going to have to keep her wits about her.

'Is my father going to be all right? This is nothing to do with his heart, is it?' A young woman, with long dark hair and pale features, hurried alongside as they wheeled the trolley towards the treatment room.

'We'll need to do some tests before we know what's causing the problem,' Jade answered. 'I'll examine your father now, and then I'll come and speak to you in a lit-tle while to keep you in the picture.'

'Thank you.' The woman allowed herself to be led away by a nurse, and Jade set about making her exam-ination.

'Is the pain bad, Rob? Can you tell me where it hurts?'

Rob Watson was clear about the pain. It had come on suddenly and it was severe, spreading throughout his abdomen and through to the back. Jade listened for bowel sounds and checked for abdominal distension and tenderness, then ordered blood tests.

'We'll do a coagulation screen as well,' she told Helen, 'and I'll need an ECG. In the meantime, we'll keep him on oxygen and give him analgesia and IV fluids. I'm going to put in a nasogastric tube and that might help relieve some of the distension.'

She looked around for a porter. 'As soon as we've finished here, we'll send him for an X-ray. That might give us more of an idea of what's going on.'

'What do you think the problem is?' Callum asked, taking her to one side a short time later.

'I can't be sure yet, but there weren't any significant abdominal findings given the severity of the pain, so I need to do more tests. His ECG shows atrial fibrillation, so I could be looking for a thrombosis or an embolism.'

Callum nodded. 'We probably need to do an angiogram. That would give us a clearer idea of what's happening. The thing to remember is that we have to be thorough and we have to be quick on this one. We can't afford to leave a possible ischaemic bowel to infarct. That would carry a high risk of mortality. Let me know what happens when he comes back from X-Ray. You should have had some of the other results back by then.'

'I will.' She hurried away to find Rob's daughter and bring her back to be with her father for a while. 'We're waiting on the results of an X-ray,' she told her, 'but it's possible that he may have suffered some kind of interruption to the blood flow to the small intestine. If that's the case, he'll need urgent surgery, but I'll keep you up to date on what's happening.'

'Thank you. You've been very kind.'

'Is there anyone who can stay with you and keep you company?' Jade asked.

The young woman shook her head. 'My mother is away at the moment. She and dad were divorced some time ago, but I still keep in touch with him. I was with my dad when he was taken ill, but I might not be able to stay. As soon as his second wife gets here, I'll probably leave. She doesn't like me, and I must say I feel the same about her.'

'I'm sorry. I know it must be difficult for you, but you could wait in another room if you want me to keep you informed.'

'Could I?' The girl looked relieved. 'That might be the best option. I'd hate to leave him and not know what's happening.'

The porter brought the patient back to the treatment room just then, and Jade hurried to look at the X-ray film. Callum came to study it with her, and said, 'There's some dilatation here. I think we should proceed to urgent angiography and start him on broad-spectrum antibiotics.'

She nodded and hurried away to call for a vascular surgeon. When she returned to her patient she discovered that his daughter had left the room and another woman was standing by the bedside. She was looking for somewhere to place her handbag and it looked as though she had only just arrived.

'Hello. Are you Mrs Watson?' Jade asked.

The woman nodded, her jaw tight. 'Are you the doctor in charge of my husband's case? What's happening to him? He was fine when I left for work first thing this morning, but look at him now. I can't believe that he's in this state.'

Jade could see that she was agitated, so she drew her away from the bedside and quietly explained the situation. 'It looks as though your husband has a blockage in an artery that supplies blood to the small intestine. We have to act quickly to restore the blood flow. We're doing everything we can to ensure his recovery.'

'But you're not…you're not giving him adequate care at all, are you? I've only just come into this room, and even I can see that one of his tubes isn't connected properly. How can I trust you to do the right thing for him?'

Jade looked over to her patient, a frown indenting her brow. Just as the woman had said, the IV tube had been disconnected. Bewildered, she called Helen over to the bedside.

'Helen, have you been in here the whole time?' she asked worriedly.

'Mostly. I had to go and get some supplies, but I was only out of the room for a minute or two.' She studied the IV tube and appeared shocked. 'That couldn't possibly have been disconnected by accident.'

'Is something wrong here?' Callum appeared in the doorway.

'Yes, there is,' the woman said. 'I don't want this doctor treating my husband. She hasn't even checked that everything is being done properly. That tube is just hanging loose.'

Jade said, 'I'll see to it.' She started to try put matters right, but Callum quickly intervened.

'No, I'll deal with this. You should go and take a break. I'll come and talk to you in a while.'

Jade stared at him, the colour draining from her face. Did he really believe that she was responsible for what had happened? Why else was he taking her off the case?

She turned, stumbled out of the room and made her way blindly towards the doctors' lounge. How could this be happening to her? This was the third time that her patients' care had been compromised, and whereas the first two incidences might have been passed off as accidental mishaps, this one certainly couldn't.

They were her patients and her responsibility. How was she to plead her innocence? She couldn't even begin to imagine how it had come about.

Callum came to the doctors' lounge some half an hour later. Jade was sitting in a chair by the table because her legs were too weak to hold her. Her hands were shaking as he came towards her, but she pressed her fingers into the fabric of her skirt and hoped that he wouldn't notice. Her gaze flicked to him.

He was straight-backed, unsmiling, but he said, 'Have you had some coffee?'

She shook her head, but couldn't bring herself to speak.

'I'll get some for both of us.' He went over to the filter machine and poured coffee into two mugs, stirring in sugar and cream.

Coming back to the table, he pushed one of the mugs towards her and then sat down opposite her. 'I have to say something to you, and I'm afraid it isn't going to be what you want to hear.'

She wrapped her fingers around the mug, but daren't pick it up for fear that her hands would shake too much.

He said quietly, 'You have to understand that I'm not apportioning blame, but I do have to take you off patient care for a time while we try to find out what's been going on.' He waited for her to absorb that, and when she didn't speak he went on, 'We could perhaps overlook the first two incidents, but this is much more serious, and it's important that we find out how it came about. I've spoken to Mrs Watson, and she's prepared at the moment to hold off from making a complaint, as long as we undertake a thorough investigation.'

He studied her for a moment in silence and then said, 'I've glanced through the files, and it looks as though you were the one consistent factor in all three incidents. The nurses who assisted were not present at all three occurrences, and there was no one else in attendance on each case as far as we can tell, except for myself as the one in overall charge.'

She found her voice at last, but it came out as a thready sound. 'So, you're saying that I'm implicated… I'm under suspicion.'

'I'm saying that I have to investigate what happened, and that while I'm doing that I have take you off any kind of work that involves interaction with patients. What I propose to do is to ask you to work on updating patients' files and perhaps outline some specific cases for presentation at a later date.'

'In case it goes to court? Is that what you're saying?'

'I don't think it will come to that.'

She gave him a flickering glance. 'When does this start?'

'Right now.'

'I see.' She moistened her lips with the tip of her tongue. 'And my patient…Mr Watson?'

'He's undergoing surgery right now. It looks as though he's suffered a mesenteric ischaemia, but I'm hoping that we've managed to catch it before it's too late.'

'Then some good might have come out of today.' She clamped her lips shut in order to stop them from trembling.

'I have to go back to my patients,' he said, pushing back his chair. 'You should go home, Jade. Take some time out to try to get over this. You've had a lot to contend with lately.'

Perhaps he thought she had not been thinking straight. With so much on her mind, it would be all too easy for her to make mistakes, and put her patients at risk. Did he really believe that?

Inside, she was crying out for him to understand that she had done nothing wrong, but she wasn't going to plead with him for that understanding. If he cared for her, he would believe in her, wouldn't he? She wanted, more than anything, for him to put his arms around her and hold her close, and tell her that everything was going to be all right, but he couldn't do that, could he?

She had tried so hard not to grow to love him, but now she realised that it was too late. She loved him and needed him, but he wasn't going to be there for her. She was on her own.

CHAPTER NINE

'I've been looking everywhere for you,' Sam said with a frown, putting his head around the door of the doctors' lounge. 'I couldn't believe it when Helen told me what happened. Is it true that you've been taken off duty?'

Jade was sitting at the table, going through a pile of paperwork, but now she looked up and nodded, her expression bleak. 'It's true. I've not been suspended as such, but I'm supposed to be updating files for the time being.'

He came into the room and she looked at him closely, her brows drawing together. There was a small tracing of blood along his forearm, and some of it had dripped onto his shirt. 'What have you done to your arm?'

He grimaced. 'It's a dogbite. Nothing too serious, but more of a warning nip, I think. We were called out to attend a man who had taken a fall at his home, and his dog didn't want to let us in. My partner's all right, but I caught the brunt of it.'

Jade stood up and went to take a closer look. 'You should have that cleaned and a dressing put on it.' She winced. 'I'm not allowed to do it for you myself, but we can go along and ask one of the nurses to patch you up. Come on, we'll go and see who's free just now. I expect Katie will be able to see to you.'

Katie went with them to the treatment room, and set about cleaning the wound for him. 'It isn't too deep,' she said, 'but you have to be careful that it doesn't become infected.' She glanced at Jade. 'What do you think? Could we get away without sutures?'

Jade nodded. 'He should have some antibiotic cover, though, and a tetanus jab, to be on the safe side. You'll have to ask Dr Franklin to sort that out.'

Katie shook her head. 'It's just awful that you've been taken off duty like this, Jade. I'm so sorry this is happening to you. We all know that you couldn't have done anything to harm the patients, but I don't know how we're going to get to the bottom of it.'

'I don't have any idea either.' Jade gave her a weak smile. 'Thanks for believing in me anyway.'

If only Callum would do the same. Since he had spoken to her yesterday about it, he had been elusive, and she would have given anything to have him come and say that he had faith in her, that everything would turn out all right. He couldn't do that, of course, and instead, she felt as though her stomach was leaden.

Katie finished the cleaning process. 'I'll go and find Dr Franklin and ask him to write up the prescription for you,' she told Sam, 'and then I'll come back and give you the tetanus shot.'

'Thanks, Katie.' Sam watched her leave the room and then turned to look at Jade. 'I'm really sorry that you're having to go through this,' he said. 'You must know that we're all in your corner.'

'It's good to know that.' Even so, until the real per-petrator was brought out into the open, she was under a cloud, and just now she couldn't see any way out.

'It doesn't make any sense to believe that you could have had anything to do with causing a patient harm. You've helped so many people. Just look at Natalie…if you hadn't acted so quickly, she might have lost the baby, but as it is, they're both doing really well. The baby's even started to put on a little weight.'

'Has he? The fact that they came through it all right was all Callum's doing really. He showed me what to do.' She glanced at Sam. 'It sounds as though you've seen Natalie since she went to the maternity ward.'

His cheeks showed a brief tinge of colour. 'I have. I went to see how she was doing, and she's looking much brighter than she was. I felt sorry for her. Her boyfriend ditched her, and then she was attacked in a horrific way. I just had to go and tell her that the man who assaulted her is going to pay for his actions.'

'I imagine she must have been happy to hear that.' Jade darted him a quick look. 'Are you going to see her again?'

Once more there was that tell-tale rush of colour to his face. 'Yes, I am. We get along really well. It's as though we just clicked somehow.'

'I'm pleased for you,' Jade said. It was good that something was going right in the world.

Katie came back just then with Dr Franklin, and Jade said goodbye to Sam and started back towards the doc-tors' lounge. As she turned to go along the corridor, Callum caught up with her.

'Jade, can I talk to you for a moment?'

She glanced at him, her eyes widening, partly with apprehension and partly with a need to know that there was some news. 'Is it about what happened with Mr Watson's IV tube? Have you learned something?'

'No, I'm sorry. There's no news yet, I'm afraid. You probably know that he came through surgery all right?'

'Yes, I heard. I'm pleased about that.' Her shoulders slumped a little. 'I was just on my way to the doctors' lounge. Do you want to talk to me in there?'

He nodded, walking alongside her and stopping to push open the door as they reached the lounge.

'I thought you would want to know that I made some headway with that other problem you had.' He looked into her eyes. 'I've managed to find out where your father is living.'

She stared at him. 'Really? That was quick. To be honest, I hadn't really expected anything to come of it.'

'I wasn't sure myself. As it happened, though, I approached the missing persons agencies and gave them your father's details as far as I knew them. And it turns out that he's living not too far away from here. It's about a forty-mile drive.'

She needed a moment or two to take it all in. 'Did you actually get in touch with him?'

He shook his head. 'I thought that step should be left up to you. I have a phone number for you, and you could make the first move, if you feel up to it.'

'I'll have to think about it.'

'I understand.' He handed her a piece of paper, and when she looked at it she saw that her father's name and address and phone number were written there.

'Thank you.' She looked up at him, her gaze troubled. 'I didn't really think that you would go through with it, given what's happened. Why would you want to do this for me?'

'I think it's important that you deal with your past. You won't be the person you need to be until you've come to grips with what's haunting you.'

'You're wrong. I don't need to know my father. I've managed without him for this long, and I can go on getting by without him.'

He reached out and circled her arms with his hands. 'You don't have to do everything on your own, Jade. At some point you're going to have to put your trust in someone else, and you'll realise that you can't always be self-reliant. Life doesn't work that way.'

'Doesn't it?' She looked at him steadily. 'I'd say, with all that's going on right now, I'm pretty much on my own, wouldn't you?'

'Jade, you—'

'Callum, we need you out here right away.' Helen pushed open the lounge door and looked into the room, adding, 'It's a cardiac arrest.'

'I'm on my way.' Callum threw a quick glance in Jade's direction. 'I'll talk to you again later,' he said. 'You should ring your father.'

Jade stared down at the piece of paper in her hands. After all this time she could hardly believe that her father was living such a short distance away. Why hadn't he ever tried to get in touch? Didn't he care anything at all for her? How could he have left behind such a small child, a child who was no older than Rebeccah, a child who had cried herself to sleep night after night because her father had never come home, because her father hadn't wanted her?

The questions circled endlessly in her head, and she almost tossed the paper in the waste bin. Almost… But then it came to her in a flash that if she did that, there would never be an end to those niggling uncertainties. Despite all her denials, they would continue to plague her, on and on. It would be better to deal with it now, once and for all, even if the outcome turned out to be not what she wanted. If she didn't do it now, she would never do it at all.

She went over to the phone and dialled the number. She heard the ring tone, and then a man's voice answered. 'Lewis Matthews.'

Her heart began to thud. The surname was different from hers, of course. Her stepfather had adopted her, and she had left her former name behind, so that now the connection between them seemed even further away.

Her mouth and throat were dry as parchment, and he must have wondered at the silence because he said, 'Hello, who's there?'

'I'm Jade,' she said. 'I'm your daughter.'

It was his turn to be silent, and she could only wonder at his reaction. Was he getting ready to put the phone down, to deny all knowledge of her? But then he said in an oddly cracked voice, 'Jade, is it really you? After all this time?'

It was a stilted conversation that followed, but she spoke to him for several minutes, telling him where she worked and that her mother was in hospital. 'I'm taking her home later today,' she said. She didn't ask him why he hadn't kept in touch, and he didn't volunteer the information. It was as though they were both shell-shocked.

She said huskily, 'I have to go now.' She left him her phone number and address and cut the call. It was all too much for her, but she had made the first contact and now the rest was up to him.

Later that day she collected her mother from the hospital ward and helped her into the car. 'You must take things easy when we get home,' she told her. 'The children will be there for a while, but then they're going off with Ben to visit Gemma, so you'll be able to get some rest.'

'I've been looking forward to this for a long time.' Her mother glanced at her, a crooked line working its way into her brow. 'You're not yourself,' she said. 'What's wrong?'

'There's been a problem at work,' Jade said briefly. 'Some of my patients were put at risk because procedures weren't done properly or the equipment was tampered with. I'm afraid it looks as though I'm the prime suspect for the moment, but Callum's looking into it.'

Her mother placed her hand on hers briefly. 'Then it will all turn out all right,' she said. 'He'll sort it all out, I'm sure of it.'

Jade gave a weak smile. Her mother had only met Callum recently, but she clearly had boundless faith in him.

'We'll see.' They were approaching the cottage now, and Jade manoeuvred the car into the drive. 'There was one other thing.' She sent her mother a swift glance. 'Callum found out where my dad is living and I called him earlier today.'

'Good heavens.' Her mother blinked. 'Are we likely to hear from him again?'

'I don't know.'

They went inside the house, and a few minutes later, just as Jade had settled her mother in the living room of the cottage, Ben arrived with the children.

Rebeccah flung her arms around her grandmother's neck. 'Nanna, you're home. I've been waiting for you to come home. Are you feeling better?'

'I am…much better, thanks.'

Connor came for a cuddle, too, and said, 'Have you seen our kitten? He's going to live with us at our house when we go back there.'

'He's beautiful, isn't he?' The kitten jumped up on to her lap, and she stroked his soft fur.

Some half an hour later Ben and the children left for the hospital, and Jade made a start on preparing the evening meal.

The doorbell rang as she was putting the casserole dish into the oven, and her mother said, 'I'll get it.'

A moment later, Jade heard the sound of voices, her mother's startled 'Hello, Callum' followed by 'Oh, my word'.

Jade shut the oven door and went to see what was going on. As she went into the hallway she saw Callum's tall figure first of all, and then, behind him, another man. The stranger was in his fifties, she guessed, and he was dark haired, clean-shaven and had eyes that were an intense grey-blue.

Callum shot her a quick glance and said, 'I thought it might be easier all round if I came and introduced Lewis to you. He called at my house first, to thank me for seeking him out, but we all know it's really you and your mother that he wants to see.'

Jade was too startled for words, but she waved a hand towards the living room and indicated that they should follow her in there.

'Mum, you should sit down and rest,' she managed at last. 'You're only just home from hospital. Go and settle yourself on the settee.'

Her mother did as Jade had suggested. Looking at Lewis, she said, 'Perhaps you should sit down, too. We have a lot of catching up to do.'

He nodded, looking a little awkward. 'That's true.' He studied her. 'I was sorry to hear about your accident. I hope you're recovering well?'

'I am.'

He turned to Jade, and he was hesitant, looking at her as though he couldn't believe his eyes. 'You must be Jade,' he said. 'Here you are, all grown up. I can't believe that so many years have gone by since I last saw you.'

'I don't think that's my fault,' she said, 'or my mother's.'

Callum said quietly, 'Perhaps I should go and leave you all to talk?'

'No,' her mother intervened. 'Please, don't go. You were good enough to help bring us all together, and I think you should stay.' She glanced at Jade for confirmation, and Jade gave a brief, slight nod.

'I'll go and put the kettle on,' she said, turning to walk out of the door.

Callum stopped her. 'I'll do it. You stay and talk to your father.' He laid a hand on her shoulder, and Jade felt the heat surge through her whole body.

She would have resisted him, but he looked into her

eyes, compelling her to stay, and she mouthed silently, 'I can't do this.'

'Trust me,' he said softly.

She gazed back at him, her eyes bright with the glint of unshed tears. How could she trust him when he was working against her, when he had no faith in her and she was being left to struggle on alone, and her career was being weighed in the balance?

In the end, though, her inner core of strength stood her in good stead. She drew in a shuddery breath and turned around and went to face her parents.

She looked at her father and said quietly, 'I was five years old when you left, and the last thing I remember saying to you was, "Please don't go."' She pressed her lips together. 'I knew that you couldn't stay, just then, but I thought you would come back. I thought you loved me, but when you stayed away I knew that it had all been a sham.'

'I planned on coming back,' he said. 'I never meant to break off the contact between us.'

Her gaze was steady. 'Then what happened to make you change your mind?'

'I didn't change my mind.' He shook his head. 'I was making one of my regular jungle treks, testing out a route for the travel company I was working for, and one day I was bitten by a snake. The man who was with me managed to get me to hospital, and they treated me, but the wound became infected and I went down with some kind of virus that turned out to be resistant to treatment. I was ill for a long time, and I had to stay in hospital for over a year.'

Her mother frowned. 'I had no idea. I wrote to your

company to find out whether you were still working for them, but they just gave me the address where you were supposed to be living. They were being taken over, and things were a bit disorganised.'

He grimaced. 'I lost my apartment because my illness went on for so long. When I was finally allowed home, I was very disorientated. I was still very weak, and everything was a struggle. I didn't even have a job because I had been on sick leave for so long. It was another two years before I was properly back on my feet. I'd been sending cards to you during those two years, but there was never any reply, and I thought that you didn't want to know me any more.'

Callum came in with the tea and handed cups around. Jade turned to her mother. 'I don't remember any cards after my fifth birthday.'

'That's because we didn't get them.'

Her father nodded. 'I realised that, much later on. I checked and found that you weren't living at your old address any longer, and there was no record of where you had gone.' He glanced at Jade. ' It didn't occur to me that your mother had married again, and that your name had changed. I kept on trying to find you, but all the time I was looking for you in the wrong surname. It was only a few days ago, when you phoned and told me that Callum had been searching for me, that I finally realised where I had gone wrong.'

Callum said, 'I'm glad that we managed to find you in the end. Jade has lived most of her life with the idea that you simply abandoned her, and yet it must have been hard on all of you from the sound of things.'

'The divorce was upsetting,' her mother said, 'but that was just the beginning of it.'

Her father grimaced. 'I was very young and inconsiderate in those days, I admit. I wanted to travel, and the thought of staying in one place and putting down roots was alien to me. I've changed now, of course.' He smiled. 'When I finally managed to get myself together, I retrained and now I work as a business consultant.'

Some time later Callum said that he had to leave, and Jade saw him out to the door. 'How do you feel now that you know the truth of the situation?' he asked.

'I don't think it's quite sunk in yet,' she admitted. 'I suppose it changes everything. He wanted to keep in touch but couldn't manage it.'

'It means that he did care for you all along. You've tried to go it alone all this time, and it's made you a stronger person, but what you have to realise is that sometimes there's no harm in letting yourself trust in other people.'

'I'm not sure about that.' Her gaze meshed with his. 'Sometimes you want to believe someone is there for you, but the reality isn't always palatable.'

'Do you think I've let you down?'

She sucked in a sharp, painful breath. 'You're doing what you have to do. You're in charge, and you have to make sure that everything is as it should be. I don't blame you for that. It's just that I feel as though I've lost out somewhere along the line.'

He bent his head towards her and kissed her lightly on the mouth. 'Try to believe in me,' he said softly. 'I'll be there for you, Jade, I promise.'

Her eyes widened in surprise. She hadn't expected that kiss, but now it lingered, searing her lips with flame and making her yearn for something more, something that was out of reach. He turned away, and she was left to watch him stride along the pathway until he was out of sight.

The next evening, her mother was flushed, in a state of barely suppressed excitement. 'I hope I'm doing the right thing,' she said. 'I don't know what made me agree to have dinner with your father.' She smoothed down her skirt and checked her image in the hall mirror. 'Do you think I look all right?'

'You look lovely,' Jade told her. 'That shade of blue suits you, and the whole outfit is very light and summery.' She helped out with the clasp of a necklace. 'Now, you remember to take it easy,' she said. 'You're still convalescing.'

'I will. I think your father understands that. He's being very considerate.' She paused, thinking about that. 'You know, he's changed a lot over the years…and for the better, it seems.'

Jade smiled. 'Yes, you're probably right.'

Connor came to inspect his grandmother's outfit. 'I've brought you a flower,' he said. 'You're s'pposed to put it in your buttonhole.'

Her mother sniffed the delicate rose petals. 'It smells beautiful,' she said. 'I'll go and wrap the stem in some damp cotton wool, and then I'll add some foil to keep it fresh.'

'My mummy likes roses,' Rebeccah said, coming to watch how it was done. 'Daddy says we'll take her some tonight…and he says we'll get the house ready for her for when she comes home.'

'She's coming home soon,' Connor put in. 'And she says we can have the kitten at home then…but for now he has to stay here.'

Jade's father knocked at the door and just a little while later they all went outside to wave her parents off. Connor was still holding the kitten, but before they had the chance to go back inside the house Ben arrived and Connor handed his furry bundle over to Rebeccah so that he could go and greet his father.

'Are we going to see Mummy?' Connor asked, and Ben nodded.

'Yes, she'll be waiting for us, wondering where we are.'

'That's 'cos you're late, aren't you?' Rebeccah said. 'Where was you?'

'Well,' Ben said, looking from one to the other, 'I was going to tell you about this later, but seeing that you're so eager to know everything… I've been sorting out a new job so that I don't have to work away from home any more.'

The children's eyes widened. 'What new job?' Connor asked. 'What is it?'

Ben looked across at Jade, and then back at the children. 'I'm going to train as a sports instructor…mostly swimming and diving, but other things as well. I've signed on for the course today.'

'That's really good news,' Jade said. 'You've always been good at sports. Is there going to be a job at the end of it?'

He nodded. 'I already have the main qualification

and some of the teaching units. This course is just a re-fresher for the teaching certificate part of it. I've had a word with the manager at the watersports centre, and there's a job lined up for me. I just have to work out my notice on the rig, and I'm home free.'

Jade smiled. 'Gemma's going to be thrilled…or does she already know about it?'

'She knows that I was thinking about it. Tonight I can present her with the done deal.' He smiled, and then looked down at the children, who were hopping about joyfully on the pavement. 'Are you two ready? Shall we go and leave Auntie Jade in peace for a while?'

'Yes, we're ready.' Rebeccah whooped and forgot that she was holding onto the kitten. 'I've lost him,' she said. 'He's run away.'

'I'll go after him,' Jade promised. 'You go and say hello to your mummy for me.'

She waved them all off, and when the car had disap-peared out of sight along the country lane she went to look for the kitten. The last time she'd seen him he'd been heading towards Callum's back garden, and now, when she came to listen, she could hear a faint mewl-ing, as though he had managed to get himself caught up somewhere.

She went and knocked on Callum's door. Her shift had finished a little earlier than his, but surely he should be home from work by now.

He opened the door a moment later, and she saw that his hair was glistening faintly, as though he had just stepped out of the shower. He was dressed in smart cas-ual clothes, dark trousers that fitted over his hips to perfection and a loose cotton shirt that smelt as though it was freshly laundered.

'Jade… I was just about to come round and see you.' He smiled, his mouth tilting in a way that made her insides melt. 'Come through to the living room. The patio doors are open to let a breeze through, and I've made up a jug of iced juice. This summer heat is way more than we expected, isn't it?'

She followed him along the wide hallway. 'I think the kitten is around the back,' she said. 'The children were worried about him. They've just gone off to the hospital to see their mother, and I said I would come and find him.'

'I thought I caught a glimpse of him. He was headed for the summerhouse, the last I saw of him. I expect he's tumbled into one of the clay pots out there.'

They walked out to the summerhouse and, sure enough, the kitten was peeping out from a big white pot, looking thoroughly confused. Callum scooped him up, and said, 'I'll pop him in a laundry basket in the kitchen. He can make himself cosy in there while we talk.'

When the kitten was safely bedded down, with a saucer of milk to hand, he closed the kitchen door and showed Jade into the living room.

It was a long, wide room with a central archway that added to the beauty of the design. There were smaller arches with glass shelves decorated with Italian glass ornaments and vases in soft shades of blue, while the same blue was picked out in various pieces set out around the room.

Jade gazed at everything, her mouth dropping in wonder. There were two sofas and a glass-topped coffee-table at one end of the room, close to the patio doors, while the other end of the room housed an elegant set of bookshelves, along with a home office, where people could sit and do paperwork or curl up in the armchair and listen to music.

'What do you think of it?' Callum asked, watching her expression.

'It's stunning,' she said. 'It's perfect.'

'I'm glad you like it.' He walked over to the sofa and patted one of the cushions. 'Come and sit down. I want to go over something with you.'

Puzzled, she did as he asked. 'Is this about work?'

He nodded, and came and sat next to her on the sofa. 'Don't look so worried. It's all right.' He poured some juice for her and handed her the glass.

'Is it?' She frowned. 'How can it be? I'm still relegated to updating files, and I'm still under a cloud.'

'I asked you to have faith in me, didn't I?' He looked at her, his head tilted slightly to one side, as though he would read her mind and unlock her defences. 'Do you remember, after the incident with the oxygen supply that was switched off, I said that we would set up some security measures?'

She nodded, and then sipped at her juice. 'I think so. You said that we would need to be extra-vigilant. I tried, but I can't watch every patient every single minute. I can't account for every instant that I'm not with them.'

'But I can.'

She looked at him oddly. 'You can? How? I don't understand.'

'One of the measures I took was to set up a closed-circuit television system. It's a little similar to the video monitoring we do when we want to do something like video conferencing or provide trainee videos for medical students.'

He paused. 'We set it up discreetly, so that no one really noticed what was going on, and we issued notices, so that patients, or relatives on their behalf, could opt out of being filmed if they wanted. Some of the notices were handed out as patients came in for treatment, and others were posted at various points throughout the department. Mostly the cameras went unnoticed, and the staff were so busy that they simply forgot they were there.'

She frowned and put her glass down on the table. 'I remember something being said about that at a meeting, but it was all so low key that we didn't take much notice. Didn't you say at the time that we might use some of the footage for training purposes?'

'That's right…provided that we had permission from patients, of course.'

She suddenly realised where all this was leading. 'Are you saying that the incident with the IV tube was filmed?'

'I am.' He smiled. 'It's taken a while for me to be able to get back to you on this because the security people had to go through the footage to find the exact moment. In the end, we've been able to discover who was behind the incident.'

'Tell me.' She was beginning to have trouble with her breathing. Was she actually in the clear? Was this going to turn out to be some kind of fluke? Her heart was thumping hard.

'Do you remember the patient who died after suffering a subarachnoid haemorrhage?'

'Stephen. His father said he had been playing squash the day before and that he was very fit? Yes, I remember. I felt awful, because I hadn't been able to treat him before the aneurysm burst. The surgeon operated on him, and we thought he might recover, but unfortunately he died of a stroke.'

'That's the one. Well, his father was very unhappy about the outcome, and somehow he had it in his head that his son should have been diagnosed earlier. It was totally impossible, of course. You did everything that you could and, in fact, some doctors might even have missed the diagnosis. We don't always think it's necessary to do a CT scan for someone presenting with a headache.'

'I still don't see how he's connected with what happened to my patient with the IV line.'

'Bear with me just a little. We know that he was responsible for what happened because he was caught on camera disconnecting the tube, but the police are still questioning him about it. We think that he had trouble accepting what had happened to his son, and that he wanted someone to blame. His grief turned to anger and it may have unhinged him, so that he decided to make you suffer for it. In his mind, you were the one who hurt his son, and he wanted to make sure that you were placed in a position where you could be blamed for what happened to your patients.'

She shook her head. 'It doesn't make any sense. How could he be sure that I would be blamed? How did he manage to do it without anyone seeing him?'

'I don't think he could guarantee that you would get the blame, but he made sure to pick out only your patients. The reason he wasn't noticed was that he put on a porter's jacket and kept his head down when there were people around.'

She put her hands to her head to calm her throbbing temples. 'It seems incredible. Didn't he have any thought for what might happen to those poor patients? In blaming me, he was hurting them.'

'As I say, I think he became unhinged, and suffered a temporary psychosis. We won't know, of course, until a psychiatrist has seen him, and the police still have to interview him some more. All I can add is that he has suffered some setbacks in the last few months. Apart from his son dying suddenly that way, there has been another loss in his family…his father, I think…and there were marriage problems. I'd say what he had been going through was probably enough to unbalance anyone. The police say that his neighbours have reported some odd behaviour on his part in recent months.'

She ran the tip of her tongue over her lips. 'It's all so hard to take in. I've been feeling as though I was being judged, and I felt that I was on my own. It's been such a difficult time.'

'I know.' He slid his arm around her shoulders. 'I wanted to tell you that it was all going to be all right, but I didn't want to say anything until we knew for certain. I hoped that you would trust me to take care of things for you.'

'I didn't know what to think.'

He drew her close to him. 'I would never let you down, Jade. I want you to know that I'll always be there for you.'

'Will you?'

'Of course I will.' He leaned towards her and kissed

her gently on the mouth. 'Why do you think I went out and found your father for you? I wanted you to be at peace with yourself and learn to trust others. You're not alone. I'm going to be by your side for as long as you want me. I just needed you to know that you don't have to do everything on your own. You can have help along the way.'

She smiled up at him, her mouth still tingling from that kiss. 'Is that why you helped out with the children and took us to the castle fête?'

'I wanted to be with you. I wanted to see you relax and enjoy a day out…and I knew the children needed it, too. I've been amazed at the way you've coped, taking on the burden of looking after them, without ever complaining. And I gave you such a hard time at the beginning.' He smiled into her eyes. 'I'm sorry about that.'

'Are you?' She returned the smile. 'You said my head was in dreamland and the children were out of control.'

'What did I know about anything? I thought you were a vision. You were the most stunning girl ever to cross my path, and you were actually going to be living next door to me, and I didn't know how I was going to handle it. When I saw that you had children, I thought that you must be married, and I hated the man who had managed to win your love. I wanted to be in his place.'

She laughed softly. 'Is that why you were such a grump? I was trying to avoid you because I thought we would be thrown out on our ears, and I was desperate for the children to behave.' She reached up and lightly stroked his face with her fingertips. 'But then I started to fall in love with you. I thought I stood no chance because you were my boss and you thought I was hopeless, and I was afraid to let myself care, because I thought I would be heartbroken if you didn't return my love.'

He pulled in a sharp breath. 'I didn't think I would ever hear you say that.' He ran his hand gently along the length of her bare arm. 'I was hard on you to begin with, I know. I was finding myself more attracted to you as the days went by, and I didn't know how I was going to be able to work with you and keep my hands off you.' He drew her close, folding his arms around her. 'And then there was Sam, forever trying to chat you up. I wanted him out of there, well away from you.' He smiled into her eyes. 'I wanted you all to myself.'

He bent his head and claimed her lips once more, his arms circling her, enfolding her and crushing her to him. 'I love you,' he said. 'I want you to be by my side for ever. I want to know that you'll wake up beside me in the mornings and be there for me every single day of the rest of our lives.'

'That's exactly what I was thinking.' She smiled and returned his kiss. 'I love you so much.'

'You don't know how much it means to me to hear you say that. I'll never let you down.' He cupped her face with his palm. 'Will you marry me, Jade?'

'Oh, yes.' She gave a tremulous sigh. 'That's a very definite yes.'

She gave herself up to his kiss, delighting in the sheer joy of having him hold her and caress her, and it was a long, long while before they came up for air.

MILLS & BOON®

Live the emotion

Tender
romance™

THE CATTLE BARON'S BRIDE *by Margaret Way*

The wilderness of the Australian Northern territory was no
place for city beauty Samantha Langdon. Cattleman Ross
Sunderland wouldn't have agreed to act as guide if he'd known
Sam would be on the trip – he'd vowed to avoid her. But with
danger and beauty all around them, their passion could no
longer be denied…

THE CINDERELLA FACTOR *by Sophie Weston*

The French chateau is the perfect hiding place for Jo – until
its owner, reporter Patrick Burns, comes home… At first
Patrick thinks the secret runaway is a thief, until he sees that
Jo is hiding her painful past. Soon she is a woman he can't live
without. But will her frightening new feelings for Patrick make
Jo run again?

CLAIMING HIS FAMILY *by Barbara Hannay*

Erin has taken her little boy to the Outback to meet his father
– her ex-husband, Luke – whom she hasn't seen for five years.
Erin is not sure how to act around the man she once loved
so deeply. Can Erin find the courage to give their marriage a
second chance – and let them become a family again?

WIFE AND MOTHER WANTED *by Nicola Marsh*

Brody Elliott is a single dad struggling to bring up his
daughter Molly. He's determined to protect his little girl from
heartbreak again. So when Molly befriends their pretty new
neighbour, Carissa Lewis, Brody is wary. If only Brody was
willing to let go of his past and give in to their attraction,
maybe Carissa could be his too…

On sale 5th May 2006

0406/02

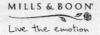

MILLS & BOON®

Live the emotion

_Medical
romance™

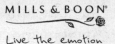

Part basset, part beagle, all Cupid... can a matchmaking hound fetch a new love for his owner?

For Nina Askew, turning forty means freedom – from the ex-husband, from their stuffy suburban home. Freedom to have her own apartment in the city, freedom to focus on what *she* wants for a change. And what she wants is a bouncy puppy to cheer her up. Instead she gets…Fred.

Overweight, smelly and obviously suffering from some kind of doggy depression, Fred is light-years from perky. But for all his faults, he does manage to put Nina face-to-face with Alex Moore, her gorgeous younger neighbour...

On sale 5th May 2006
Don't miss out!

Available at WHSmith, Tesco, ASDA, Borders, Eason, Sainsbury's and all good paperback bookshops

www.millsandboon.co.uk

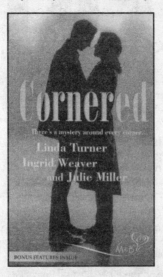

4 FREE

BOOKS AND A SURPRISE GIFT!

We would like to take this opportunity to thank you for reading this Mills & Boon® book by offering you the chance to take FOUR more specially selected titles from the Medical Romance™ series absolutely FREE! We're also making this offer to introduce you to the benefits of the Reader Service™—

★ **FREE home delivery**
★ **FREE gifts and competitions**
★ **FREE monthly Newsletter**
★ **Exclusive Reader Service offers**
★ **Books available before they're in the shops**

Accepting these FREE books and gift places you under no obligation to buy, you may cancel at any time, even after receiving your free shipment. Simply complete your details below and return the entire page to the address below. You don't even need a stamp!

YES! Please send me 4 free Medical Romance books and a surprise gift. I understand that unless you hear from me, I will receive 6 superb new titles every month for just £2.80 each, postage and packing free. I am under no obligation to purchase any books and may cancel my subscription at any time. The free books and gift will be mine to keep in any case.

M6ZED

Ms/Mrs/Miss/Mr ....Initials ....
BLOCK CAPITALS PLEASE

Surname ....

Address ....

....

....Postcode................................

Send this whole page to:
UK: FREEPOST CN81, Croydon, CR9 3WZ